Assassins of a Hustla's Heart

A Deadly Divas Tale

By:

Dominique Washington

<u>Text GRANDPENZ to 22828 to stay up to date with new releases, sneak peeks, contest, and more…</u>

<u>Check your spam if you don't receive an email thanking you for signing up.</u>

Text SPROMANCE to 22828 to stay up to date on new releases, plus get information on contest, sneak peeks, and more!

Prologue

Club Push was popping. Everyone who was anyone was in the building. The night was young, but there was already a line wrapped around the building.

There was a long red carpet in front of the club, roped off. Only VIP guests were allowed to walk the red carpet. At the entrance, was a huge red and black balloon arch. The banner in front of the club read "Happy Birthday, Queen Takela."

Takela and her girls pulled up in a black on black Mercedes-Benz S-600 Pullman. They killed the scene as they stepped out and walked down the red carpet.

Takela wore a short McQ Alexander McQueen red bondage midi dress with red and black stilettos. Kayla wore a Michael Kors red lace one shoulder cut-out asymmetrical bodycon dress with matching red stilettos. Monica wore a red Dolce & Gabbana halter backless front cut-out strappy bodycon dress with matching pumps. Jaz wore a La Petite Robe di Chiara Boni red and black multi wear panty embroidered dress with black pumps. Mya wore a red Jimmy Choo lace club dress with matching Jimmy Choo pumps. Shay wore a red Vestidos Pu Leather Hollow lace backless dress with black pumps.

They killed it, and they knew it. They could see the envy and hate in the chicks' eyes as they walked past. They ate it up too. They posed for a few pictures and made their way in for Takela's grand entrance.

Inside, there were red and black balloon arches strategically placed around the club. There were photo booths setup with the Chanel theme in the background. Each table had Chanel red tablecloths and Chanel centerpieces. The elevators were decorated in the red and black Chanel theme as well. The pools were filled with red foam with red and black balloons placed in and around it.

She had personal bars setup in each VIP section, so everyone in VIP had their drinks brought to them. All drinks were free in the VIP area. There was a seafood buffet setup a few feet from the bar.

"Alright, stop what the fuck y'all doing and let's welcome one of the baddest chicks in the building!! The birthday girl!! Queen Takela!!!" the DJ announced.

The club roared in applause as Takela made her way to her throne with her name above it. Mason met Takela at the door.

"Happy birthday, baby," he said and gave her a long passionate kiss.

"Get a damn room," Monica said and smiled.

'We already got one upstairs," Mason said and winked.

They headed toward their section and took their seats. Takela wanted to scope out the scene before she hit the dance floor. She couldn't believe the turnout. She wondered if they were over the capacity. The bartender came up and took their orders for drinks.

"Let me get a Sex on the Beach," Shay said. She knew she shouldn't be drinking, but she was going to need one to make it through the night.

"I'll have what she's having," Jaz and Mya said.

"I'll have a virgin daiquiri," Takela said.

"Let me get a martini," Monica said.

"Me too," Kayla said.

The bartender nodded and left to fill their orders.

They nodded their heads and looked at the down at the dance floor. The DJ was playing Future and Drake *Used to This*.

After they had gotten a couple of drinks in their system, they were ready to hit the dance floor. When the DJ played Rihanna's *Work*, Takela pulled Mason to the dance floor. They grinded on each other as if they were fucking on the dance floor. The DJ switched it up and played Rihanna's *Love on the Brain*. Takela wrapped her arms around Mason's neck and began to rock and sing along.

At that moment, standing in his arms, she knew that was where she always wanted to be. Mason kneeled on one knee in the middle of the dance floor and took Takela's hand in his. The DJ stopped the music, and a guy walked up and handed Mason the mic.

"Takela, my queen, I have loved you since the day I met you. I'll never stop loving. You are the woman I want to spend the rest of my life with. I promise I will do everything I can to keep a smile on your face. I promise I will never intentionally harm or hurt you. Most relationships fail due to lack of communication, so I promise to always keep a line of communication open with you. You have stood by me through thick and thin. Will you marry me, my Queen Takela?" Mason asked.

"Oh my God, Mason baby, yes. It will be an honor," she said.

He slid the five-karat round, three-stone engagement ring on her finger. Everyone applauded as they exited the dance floor.

"Real man type of shit," the DJ said and turned the music back up. Mason held her in his arms as they looked out at the crowd.

POW! POW! POW!

Takela and Mason both hit the floor.

Chapter One

"Where the hell is it?" Takela asked as she frantically searched through the closet in search of the Ruger SR9 9mm. She knew time wasn't on her side as she searched. She was ready to finish the job, get paid, and go home.

Rob and kill were what she and her girls Kayla, Monica, and Shay, did best. They didn't have the time, or patience, to punch anyone's clock and wait on a check.

Her girl, Kayla, texted her, informing her that she hid the gun on the shelf in the closet. Her target was in the bathroom with an upset stomach after she put her magic potion in his drink. She couldn't understand why the nigga hadn't passed out yet. She gave him enough to sedate a damn horse, yet it only seemed to give him a stomachache at the most.

What planet is this nigga from? She said to herself.

It became crystal clear that the gun wasn't there. She had to come up with a new plan, because she refused to leave empty-handed. He was paid, and she knew it. She just had to figure out how she could get him to open his safe.

Takela heard the familiar sound of a gun cocking and felt the cold barrel pressed against her head.

"Looking for this?" Rikki asked with a smug smile.

She was so busy searching through his closet that she didn't hear the water go off or the door open.

Fuck, she thought to herself.

"Now why would I be looking for that?" she said trying to come up with a lie.

"Bitch, don't play with me," he said then smacked her with the gun.

"I ain't the average nigga. I can smell a gold-digging rat miles away. Where is the other one?" he asked, catching Takela off-guard.

"Yeah, I know you sent her," he said and laughed.

"What the fuck are you talking about?" she asked. He hit her again, even harder, opening a gash on the side of her temple.

"Like I said bitch, I ain't the average cat. I didn't make it this far by being stupid. See those cameras up there?" he asked as he pointed to the camera in the far-right corner of the room.

She hadn't even realized it was there until he pointed it out.

"My cameras record 24/7. It immediately notifies me and sends video footage when someone passes through the motion detector. I recognized her from a picture you had on your dashboard."

Takela now regretted choosing to do this job solo. Yes, she knew she was more than capable of handling her own if it came down to it. However, she didn't expect things to go to the left so quickly. She wasn't prepared for this hit. She was prepared for something a little less messy, but oh well. She just prayed her girls would burst in. They agreed not to do the job with her, but only if they could stay close to make sure she was straight. She declined and now look where she was.

"I'm gone show you hoes I'm not to be fucked with, and when I get through with you, I'm going for your little friend," he said and laughed.

He snatched her hair and dragged her out the closet. He began to beat her mercilessly with his fist and anything else in his reach. Everything in the room was a weapon that he utilized. He dragged her down the stairs, causing her to hit her head on each step.

"Bitches trying to set me up. Okay," he said as he slapped her. He went into the closet and pulled out rope and tape. After snatching her clothes off, he made her get on her knees and tied her ankles together. Then he tied her hands behind her back. He pulled an African Sjambok whipping staff from the closet.

"Chicks like you never learn," he said.

He raised the staff and came crashing down on her back like a lightning bolt. She let out an ear-piercing scream that sounded like music to his ears. He hit her again. He beat her until she passed out. He dumped ice water on her a few moments later. Then, he examined his work.

"Oh my God, girl, you got a tree on your back," he said, laughing hysterically as he quoted a line from the movie *Beloved*. Takela was in so much pain that she couldn't move. He slapped her across the back of her neck with the staff with so much force that a gash instantly opened. She screamed.

Takela had always been the tough one, not letting anyone see her weak. She would always hold her emotions in. She was taught at a very young age that showing your emotions could be fatal, so she always hid them.

He laughed and said, "Oh, we just getting started."

He had this demonic gaze that caused chill bumps to rise on her body. No matter how much pain he inflicted, she would never beg for her life. She already knew she wouldn't make it out of there alive. He took a knife and carved his initials on her back. As he made it to the last letter, he heard a loud crash come from the kitchen.

"What the fuck?" he said as he jumped up to inspect it. He grabbed his gun and walked cautiously toward the kitchen.

Takela heard someone behind her, but was too sore to move. Kayla made her way toward her. The look on Kayla's face let her know that she was fucked up. She didn't need a mirror.

"Oh my God, Takela, I am so sorry," she said as a tear fell from her eyes. "Don't worry, boo, I got you. He gone pay for this with his life."

Kayla heard Rikki approaching, and she sped off toward the closet on the opposite side of the room. Rikki had left his phone on the table, so Takela knew he didn't see Kayla enter. He went straight to the table to get his phone and Takela started to panic. As he unlocked his phone, Kayla swung the metal bat, hitting him in the head, knocking the wind out of him. Rikki instantly hit the floor. Kayla swung again, hitting him in his ribs.

"An eye for an eye," she said as she swung the bat again.

She then noticed the whipping staff laying a few feet away and picked it up.

"What type of shit is this? Who the fuck buy shit like this?" Kayla said examining the staff.

"We weren't going to kill you. Well, we were going to kill you, and we still are. It would've been quick, but you fucked up. Monica. Shay," Kayla called out. Her girls came in, and the scene before them brought them to tears.

"Take her to Dr. Adams. I'm going to stay here and finish this shit," Kayla said.

Shay and Monica carried Takela to the car. Shay reentered the house, finally gazing around. It was decked out.

"Help me," Kala told Shay.

They tied his arms and cuffed his ankles.

"Where is the money?" Kayla asked.

"Fuck you, bitch," he spat.

"I see you like doing shit the hard way," Kayla said.

She pulled out her kit. Kayla had always been fascinated with knives and what they could do. This was her preferred method. She had always been amused at how different people reacted when you pulled a gun on them, versus when you pulled a knife. People would try to overpower someone with a gun, but the thought to take the knife never crossed their minds.

Rikki didn't appear the least bit fazed when he saw the knife in her hand. She didn't say a word as she approached him and lifted his shorts over his knee. She took the scalpel, and in one swift motion, sliced his knee, exposing his bone. He screamed out in agony.

"Fuck!"

Shay went into the laundry room and returned with a bottle of bleach.

"That's what the fuck I'm talking about," Kayla yelled and laughed.

She moved to the side to allow Shay room to do what she wanted to do. Shay had always been fascinated with chemicals. She could make a bomb in under ten minutes that could blow up eight blocks. She opened the bleach and poured it into his open wound, causing him to scream and shake uncontrollably.

"Where is the money?" Kayla asked again. He stalled.

"Honey, we can do this all day," she mused.

Kayla proceeded to cut his other knee, then she snatched his shirt off him and rubbed some bleach on him. She forced him to bend over while sitting, and tied his hands to his ankles and the chair legs. With his back being exposed, Kayla swung. *Whoosh* was the sound that came from the staff before it connected with his back.

"AAGHHHHHHHHH!" Rikki screamed.

"Whew!! Don't like it when you're on the receiving end, now do you?" she asked as she swung again and again.

"Now, are you gone tell me where the stash is?" Kayla asked. When he didn't answer, she continued to beat him.

"P-p-please st-st-op. It's u-u-under the floor boards in th-the kitchen," Rikki said, barely able to speak. Rikki had $87,000 under the floor board. To them, that was nothing.

"That's it?" Shay questioned in disbelief.

"Who put you on this cat?" she asked Kayla.

"Same person as always," she said.

"Let's just get this shit, kill that motherfucker, and roll out," Shay said, pissed. After they had gotten what they came for, Kayla castrated Rikki, putting his dick in his mouth, and sliced his throat from ear-to-ear. After disabling the camera and collecting the tapes they left.

Chapter Two

Shay and Kayla pulled into Dr. Adams' driveway forty-five minutes later. Seeing Takela like that was a heartbreaking scene. She was stable. Fucked up, but stable. Her wounds would heal in time.

They all regretted agreeing to let Takela do the job alone. They knew should've, could've, and would've wouldn't help the situation, or change it. So, there was no point in crying over spilled milk.

Dr. Adams greeted them at the door and led them to the back where Takela was sound asleep.

"How is she?" Kayla asked.

"For the most part, she will live and heal, but there will be many scars. She has three broken ribs and a broken jaw. She suffered contusions and many lacerations on her back and neck. Some will heal without leaving a scar, and others won't. She also has a few broken bones. I can't speak to her mental condition yet," he said.

"Takela is very strong. Unbreakable. What doesn't kill her only makes her stronger. Besides, she's been through worse. She's a survivor," Kayla said with confidence.

"It's still fucked up that it happened to her. Never again," Monica said.

The girls huddled around her bed for an hour then they headed out. Kayla knew she had to break the news to Mason, Takela's man. He knew about their hustle and never knocked them for it. Instead of criticizing them for how they chose to get money, he decided to train them. He knew that they were going to do what they wanted to do, regardless of what he had to say.

Mason was a well-trained sniper. He took them to the outdoor shooting range and taught them how to shoot. He trained them with every kind of gun. He was one of the best, and he made sure to train them to be the best.

He trained them to defend themselves in hand-to-hand combat, and with blades. Kayla already knew he was about to get on her ass, because he told them to always work together, and never to send one woman to do a job. No matter how easy it seemed. Clearly, they'd fucked up.

She wanted to go straight home, but she knew waiting to tell him would only make it worse.

"Hey, Mason, it's Kayla," she said when Mason answered the phone.

"I can't talk right now. I'm in the middle of something important. I'll hit you back later," he said, then ended the call without giving Kayla time to protest.

"Fuck!" she said as she drove toward her home.

It had been a very long night, and she needed to sleep. As she sat in her bubble bath, she thought back to when she met her girls.

16

"Why can't I stay at my old school? I don't want to leave my friends," a twelve-year-old Kayla whined.

"Because trying to get you all the way across town every morning, then having to come back here to go to work will be a huge inconvenience. There is nothing wrong with this school, and it's walking distance. So, when you make friends, you could walk," her mom said.

"I don't want to make new friends. I don't want any friends," Kayla said.

"Stop whining and come on before you're late."

Kayla's first day at school was horrible. Everybody laughed at her red hair, light skin, freckles, and braces. They made fun of her and called her names. She wasn't mixed at all. Her mom was light-skinned, and her father had a dark complexion. Nobody in her family had freckles or red hair, as far as she knew. She was the oddball of the family.

"Mommy, I don't want to go back there," Kayla cried the next morning. "They talked about me," she cried.

"Girl, they talked about Jesus, but that didn't stop him. Baby girl, people are going to talk about you whether you are cute or ugly, up or down, or doing bad or good. No matter what you do, people will always try to find a flaw. If they can't find one, they will make up one. Never let what they say faze you. Let them talk. Let them think what they want about you. You know who you are. You are a beautiful

17

young lady, and don't let anybody tell you different. As long as you know you are beautiful, to hell with what people say. Okay? Never let people see you sweat. Never let them know what they say hurts you, even if it does. Always wear your poker face, okay baby?" her mom said.

"Okay, mommy," Kayla said, her mood lifted.

This time she walked into class with a smile on her face. She heard a few snickers, but she didn't care. That afternoon on the playground, Kayla was approached by three other students Gigi, Bre and Porsha. They were known for starting shit and teaming up on anybody they deemed weak.

"How does it feel to wake up every morning and look in the mirror just to see that looking back at you?" Gigi, the leader if the group asked. The other girls chuckled.

"It feels better to know I have this face looking back at me, instead of that," Kayla said pointing directly at Gigi's face.

"Oooohhh" and "ahhhh" came from the students around the yard. They had drawn a crowd that quickly. Gigi was furious. She was one of those kids that was too big for her age. She looked like she belonged in the ninth grade instead of the seventh.

"You little freckled face bitch, I will knock that smile right off your ugly ass face," Gigi said as she stepped in Kayla's face.

"Whoop her ass, Gigi," Bre said.

"You better get out my face," Kayla warned. Kayla wasn't a fighter, but she wasn't a runner, either. She didn't like to fight, but *that didn't mean she couldn't get down. She knew the girls would try to jump her, but she didn't care.*

"Or what?" Gigi said mushing Kayla in the face. Kayla hauled off and punched Gigi square in the nose, causing her nose to bleed.

"Bitch," Gigi said as she started to pounce on Kayla.

"Fight! Fight! Fight!" the students yelled as they surrounded the girls. Gigi swung at Kayla continuously connecting with her face. It seemed as though after the first few blows, Gigi threw on Kayla, they stopped having an impact on her. It was like Kayla was shaking them off. Kayla hit Gigi in the throat, catching her by surprise, causing her to stop swinging, and hold her neck. Kayla then started to pound her with nothing but face shots. She swung with everything she had in her.

"Aw, hell nah," Bre said as Kayla beat Gigi. She ran up, grabbed Kayla by her hair, and pulled her on the ground. She held Kayla's hair with one hand and delivered blow after blow to her face with the other one.

This didn't stop Kayla, though. She still held her own. Porsha ran up, and they both jumped Kayla. By this time, Gigi had recovered and ran up as well. Instead of swinging at Kayla, Gigi stomped her.

Out of nowhere, two girls ran up. One snatched Gigi off Kayla and delivered vicious blows to her face. She beat Gigi non-stop, not allowing her to get so much as a punch in. All Gigi could do was ball up to protect her face. The girl then pulled out a razor and sliced the right side of Gigi's face to the white meat. She sliced her hands as well.

The other girl snatched Bre, off Kayla. Instead of punching her, she wrapped her hand around Bre's hair and started ramming her head into the pole connected to the slide.

Having two of the girls off her allowed Kayla to get up and stomp Porsha. The girl that was on Gigi backed up and admired her work. Gigi was still balled up wailing. She was able to get rid of the blade before anyone saw it. Most were still trying to figure out where the blood was coming from.

"Break it up, now!" one of the teachers yelled as they ran out to break up the fight.

They managed to pull the girls apart and brought them all into the principal's office.

"Who are you?" Kayla asked the girl she saw beating Gigi.

"A thank you would be more like it. Ugh, rudeness! My name is Takela, and this chick here is Shay. We figured you could use some help," Takela said.

"Nah, I could've fought my own battles," Kayla said.

"Yeah, we could see that," Shay said, then laughed.

Kayla rolled her eyes and said, "Look, thank you for your unwanted help. I'm not a sore loser, so the loss wouldn't have got to me. I would've seen them tricks again."

"Unwanted, but clearly needed help," Takela said returning the attitude.

"Look boo, we not trying to beef with you. Them tramps had it coming. They love teaming up on people. That's all they do. Bitches just hate competition," Shay said.

"Watch your mouth," the secretary in the office said. Shay just rolled her eyes.

Each girl received a ten-day suspension. Since Kayla's mom was at work, she had to walk home.

"You're not from around here are you?" Shay asked Kayla.

"I'm from Olive Branch, Mississippi. My mom switched jobs, so we had to move," Kayla answered, unenthused.

"We live right around the corner on American Way," Kayla continued.

"That's what's up. I live on the other side, about six houses down from you. You would need to make a left to get to mines, instead of a right. I saw you guys move in. Takela lives behind us," Shay said. Takela rolled her eyes.

"Don't tell my damn business! If I wanted her to know where I stayed, I would've told her my damn self."

"Damn my bad, boo," Shay said laughing.

"As you can see, she is a real bitch, but you'll get used to it. We've been friends since we were toddlers, so my mom says. My girl Monica, too. She lives in the area too, but her ugly ass is sick today," Shay said.

The girls walked Kayla to her front door and parted ways.

Over the next few weeks, they pretty much just got to know each other. As the years passed, they were inseparable. They were a force to be reckoned with. When one fought, they all fought, and they NEVER lost a fight. They became close as sisters over the years.

Monica was by far the deadliest one. She stood five feet, six inches and weighed one hundred forty pounds. She had curves in all the right places, a caramel complexion, and big doe, honey eyes. She was as sweet as pie until you got on her bad side, and fucking with her sisters would get you there in a blink of an eye.

When she hit you, she hit hard. No one ever saw her coming until it was too late. She had this innocence about her. Her eyes were trusting, and she could lure anybody in without even trying. She could bring the strongest nigga to his knees.

Guns were her specialty. She could shoot any target, near or far. She never missed. Mason didn't have to do much to train her, because she was already well-versed. He just made her deadlier.

Shay was the more laid back one. She was always cool, calm, and collected, even when putting in work. She never panicked, no matter the situation.

Shay stood five foot, five inches and weighed one seventy. She had curves for days; a pancake-flat, small waist; and a round ass. She had long wavy hair that flowed freely down hair back. She was paper sack brown with dark brown eyes.

She had the ability to pull niggas, and chicks too. When trying to touch a nigga, her motto was to get the bitch, then the nigga will come to you. She never went looking. Her preferred killing method was poison. As a child, she would always mix different chemicals to see the reaction.

After she graduated, she went onto study chemical engineering. She also went to medical school, but didn't finish. She wanted to know all she could about medicine and human anatomy. She loved to torture her victims. Sleeping on her or any of her crew was a fatal mistake.

Takela was the bold, outspoken one. She had the smartest mouth. She didn't sugarcoat shit. She saw no point in doing so. She took no bullshit. She was the smallest of the group. She stood five feet, one inch and weighed one hundred forty-five pounds. She had dark skin, honey eyes, and shoulder-length hair. Like her girls, she had curves in all the right places.

What she lacked in height, she made up for in madness. It was best to stay on her good side. She would kill for the smallest things. She had many different killing methods. She never stuck to one. She instilled in her girls to be skilled in all areas.

"Never know when you may not be able to pull your blade or reach your gun," she would tell them.

She was the brains of the four. They all were smart, but it was her that put them together and kept them going this long. She was the head of the snake.

Kayla was the quiet one. She loved the element of surprise. Where her girls would eventually show themselves, Kayla was the type to stay hidden until the finale. You never saw her coming, literally. She still had red hair, but her freckles went away with age.

At age twenty-five, she stood five feet, six inches tall weighing one hundred-sixty pounds. She had light skin, curly red hair, brown eyes, and a body like a video vixen. She was the whole package.

Her favorite killing method was her blades. She loved to cut a nigga limb from limb. She had always been fascinated with knives and swords. She had her own personal collection of Japanese Katana Blades at her disposal.

***

The ringing of her phone brought her back to the here and now.

"Hello," she answered.

"What's up, sexy, you at home?" her man, Rocky, asked.

"Hey, babe. Yeah, I'm here. I was taking a bath," she said.

"Can I slide through?" Rocky asked.

"Of course," Kayla answered.

"Okay I'm on my way now," he said then ended the call.

"Just what I need," Kayla said as she stepped out the tub and prepared for her man's arrival.

Chapter Three

When Takela finally woke the next night, she felt as though her head was going to explode. The light in the room wasn't much help, either.

"Well, look who decided to join the land of the living," Dr. Adams said as he entered the room.

"How are you feeling?" he asked.

"Like shit. My head is pounding, and my lower half is sore."

"I can give you something for the pain. You also need to eat something. In the meantime, you have a visitor," he said as he stepped aside.

When Takela saw Mason, she wanted to disappear. She knew he was about to grill her for her poor decisions. She just waited for it. Oddly, when she looked into his eyes, she didn't see anger there.

"Hey, baby. I've been here about three hours waiting on you to wake up. Kayla told me what happened. I'll get into that later, though. I see you got fucked up pretty bad, though. One wouldn't believe you're a trained assassin," he joked, making light of the situation.

"I know, baby. Shit went to the left real quick. I'm just ready to get out of here and go home," she said.

"That's what I'm here for. We can leave once he check you again," Mason said.

***

As soon as they made it into Mason's house, he let Takela have it.

"Why the fuck is you so damned hard-headed? Didn't I tell ya ass never do a job alone? You been doing this shit too long to start making amateur fucking moves, T," he yelled. "And didn't I fucking teach y'all to never do jobs in the city where you sleep, and never revisit the city where you do the job? I don't tell y'all this shit because I like to hear myself talk. I tell y'all the shit because it works," Mason said.

He wanted to knock the shit out of all of them.

"I know, baby. I'm sorry. I-"

"T, don't be fucking sorry, be careful," he yelled, cutting her off mid-sentence.

Takela didn't feel like having that discussion right then. She was still in pain and just wanted to lay down.

As if Mason read her thoughts, he said, "Come on baby, you need to lay down. We will discuss this later," he led her to the bed. They both got in and were asleep in minutes.

***

After a few weeks, Takela and her girls were back at it. Takela still had a few scars on her back to remind her of what happened, but she didn't care. Mason loved her regardless of the scars.

She noticed that her girls were a little skeptical about her starting back so soon. They went on a few jobs without telling her. They would always bring her share when they were finished.

They all told her that they had it, and she could easily get money from sitting on her ass, but Takela wasn't having it. She had always worked for what she wanted, and this was no different. Besides, it was her connect putting them on each job. She told him to stop putting them on. When they noticed he wasn't budging, they agreed to let her in. She now, more than ever, wanted to stack her cash and relocate.

In due time, Takela, she said to herself.

Chapter Four

"This next job will require all hands on deck," Takela said.

"Tony is a very powerful man. He keeps guards around him, 24/7," Takela explained.

"You know I can handle it," Monica said.

"Of course, I know you can, but they're standing too close together. Each one of them can see the other so you wouldn't be able to take one out without alarming the others," Takela said.

"Smart move," Shay said.

"If that's the case, how are we supposed to complete the job, if we can't take out the guards?" Monica asked.

"We won't need to take out the guards because we will be in the house. Tony uses an escort service regularly. That's our way in. He requested four women," Takela explained.

"What the hell does he need with four women?" Shay asked.

"I don't know, and I don't really give a fuck, either. My concern is the money, and that's it. We gone go in there and do the job we're getting paid to do," she said.

The girls changed into some Victoria's Secret lingerie and headed for the door. Takela scoped the scene as they turned on Tony's street. She counted seven guards total outside and three inside the house, two in the back and two in the front.

Monica was skeptical about parking in the driveway because she didn't want anything linking them to the crime but after a little convincing from Takela and drive out tags being placed on the car she was ready.

"Let's get it," Takela said as they exited the car.

"Hey, papi," Kayla said using her fake Hispanic accent. They all opened trench coats, causing Tony's mouth to drop.

"Damn, baby," he said.

"Aye, Dame, you see this shit? Pick one," Tony said. Dame looked at each lady and chose Monica.

"Good choice," he said.

"Dee, which one of these hoes you want?" Tony asked. Dee chose Shay.

"That's what's up," Tony said as the men led each woman to the back.

"Y'all want something to drink?" asked Tony as he walked over to the mini bar.

"Sure. Surprise us," Takela said, answering his next question before he asked it.

He poured them a drink and went to the dresser to roll a blunt. He sat his cup down on the nightstand, giving Takela the opportunity to drop the pills in his drink without getting caught.

They both climbed on the bed and started to kiss each other while he stood back and lit his blunt. He just watched them.

Kayla took Takela's bra off and begin to suck hungrily on her nipples. Even though they were on a job, Takela couldn't help being turned on. It made her pussy wet knowing he was watching her. It didn't help that Kayla had her in a zone. Kayla then started to suck her left nipple.

"Sssssss," Takela moaned.

Kayla slid a finger inside her wetness and was immediately turned on. She started to finger fuck her while rubbing her thumb across her clit.

"Ooohhh fffucckk," Takela cried out as she came on Kayla's hand.

Kayla was taken aback. She laid Takela on her back and began to kiss her way down her body. She slid Takela's panties to the side and kissed her clit. Now Takela was taken aback. She was turned on by it, but they agreed that they would pretend to be eating pussy.

Oh well, she thought as Kayla started to slide her tongue over her walls.

"Yessss," she moaned out.

Kayla began to fuck her with her tongue. She then started to suck on her clit, causing Takela to cry out in pleasure.

"Bbbaaabbyyyy, fuckkkk yessss like that," she instructed Kayla.

Kayla slid her tongue over Takela's ass causing her to jump. She slid her tongue in and out her ass.

"Shitttt, yessss," Takela moaned.

"Ooohhhh, I'm about to cum, oohhhhh," Takela moaned as she came on Kayla's tongue.

She came so hard that her legs shook. Takela looked up to see Tony naked with his dick in his hand, watching them.

"Bring me that pussy, baby. Come ride my face," Takela said.

By this time, they both were into it. Kayla mounted Takela's face.

"Sssssss," Kayla moaned.

Takela fucked Kayla with her tongue until Kayla came. She lapped up every drop. Takela motioned for Tony to join them. He happily obliged.

The girls got into the sixty-nine position with Takela on top facing Tony. As Kayla devoured her pussy as if it was her last meal, Takela took Tony's nine inches into her mouth. She could feel him growing another inch as she began to deep throat his dick. She ran her tongue over his shaft and then she gave his balls the attention they were seeking.

"Damn. That's right. Suck this dick," he moaned. Tony started to fuck Takela's face.

"Open that throat," he told her as he attempted to shove his dick down her throat.

Takela's gag reflex was on point. She didn't gag on his dick once. As Takela climbed off Kayla, Tony buried his face in Kayla's dripping wet pussy.

"Ohhhh," she cried out. She came moments later.

Tony instructed Takela to stand as he and Kayla got on their knees in front of her. First, Tony parted Takela's legs then began to lick her pussy. He then moved back and allowed Kayla to do the same. They were driving Takela crazy. Kayla moved her head over so there would be enough room for the both of them. They both ate her pussy at the same time.

"Ohhhh my God. Fuuuucckkkkk yessss," Takela cried out.

She was in complete bliss as she squirted on both of their tongues. She knew she needed a moment to recover. As the night progressed, Takela noticed that Tony never touched his drink. She wanted to slap the shit out of Kayla when she accidently bumped into the dresser, causing the drink to spill. Kayla could see the anger in Takela's eyes, but Takela kept her cool.

Stupid bitch, she thought. As they finished up, Tony went to the bathroom to freshen up.

"Don't go nowhere. I'm looking forward to round two," he said.

As he opened the bathroom door to exit, he was met with the end of the metal pole that he kept on the side of his bar. When the pole connected with his temple, he became dazed, but he didn't fall. Before he could retaliate, Takela swung the pole again with twice as much force as the last lick. This time he hit the floor, knocked unconscious.

"Help me get this nigga to the bed," Takela said.

They used the sheets to tie him to a bar chair that was mounted in the floor. They shoved a sock in his mouth to keep him from alerting the others.

Both women began to search the room quietly. They couldn't find the safe.

"Fuck," Takela said in frustration. They were being paid a hefty fee to do the job, but they could use more. As Kayla tiptoed over to the bed, she heard the floor creak. She bent down and lifted the floor board to find a huge safe.

"Bingo," she said excitedly.

Just as Takela walked up, Tony began to stir awake. He tried to speak, but the sock had his voice muffled. They could tell he was beyond pissed by the way he looked at them. If looks could kill, they would have dropped dead ten seconds ago. Kayla surveyed the safe. She was a lock expert. *"Nothing is ever truly locked,"* is what she would say.

When she looked at the type of lock on the safe, she smiled. Tony had made her job so much easier. There was a finger print lock on the safe. She pulled her scalpel and cut his index finger off without warning. She then picked up the lighter from the dresser and burned the wound. Had Tony not been gagged, the whole neighborhood would've heard his screams.

She pressed his finger to the safe, and it opened. They looked inside in awe. There were several duffel bags filled with money and dope. They knew it had to be a little over two million in the safe. The kilos of coke could easily be worth over a hundred thousand.

After they had the safe open, they placed each bag outside of the bedroom window.

Kayla took her other scalpel and began to cut below his ribcage in an upward motion causing him to gurgle. When she reach his lungs she he started to convulse. He was going into shock as she cut through exposing his heart. His warm blood coated her face and arms. She cut his aorta and yanked his heart out with veins and arteries attached.

Takela stood back and watched. Kayla sat his heart in his lap after cutting his dick off. She removed the sock and shoved it in his mouth.

"Well, our job is done," she said.

"Not really," Takela said, remembering the guards. She hoped her girls took care of their business and were ready to roll. As they were dressing, they heard a knock on the door. They froze in place.

"I got it," Takela said. The bar area couldn't be seen from the room door, so she knew she was cool.

"Hey," she said.

"I need to holla at Tony real quick," he said. He had his hand on one of the guns he was carrying as if he sensed foul play. Takela let him in and closed the door behind him.

"He's over there," she pointed. The sight before him left him gasping for air, as if he couldn't breathe. He collected himself after a few moments and reached for his gun. Before he could grab it from the hostler, Kayla hit him with the pole. He fell on the first try.

"Weak ass nigga," she said. They took his guns from him and tried to drag him to the other side of the room. As they dragged him, Takela noticed a huge black box that could be a tool kit. When she opened it, she was amazed to see a complete arsenal of guns, bullets, grenades, and more.

"Jackpot," she said. Takela handed Kayla two guns and took two for herself as well as a few grenades.

They left the room, hiding the weapons in their coats. Just as they walked out, both Shay and Monica did as well. Neither girl killed the men, but that was okay with Takela.

"Them niggas so lame," Monica laughed as she looked back and saw Dame knocked out.

The girls made their way to the door just as it opened. They stopped mid-step. They knew they had to play it cool if they wanted to leave there alive.

"Where is Tony?" the henchman asked.

"He's in recovery," Takela stated with a naughty smile.

"He normally walks his date out. Stay right there," he said as he headed for Tony's room.

The women knew they needed to get the hell out of there fast. They ran out the door.

Takela pulled the pin off one the grenades and tossing it towards the other side of the house so she could distract the men.

When the guards ran towards the blast the women collected the bags and ran towards the car. Before Takela ran off she through a grenade insides the window they left partially open. She threw two more over her shoulders as she ran to the car.

"The job is done," Takela spoke into the phone.

"Okay. I'm wiring the money to your account now. Thank you for your services," the man said. She checked the account, and sure enough, it was there.

"Time to go home. Memphis, here we come," Kayla said as they high-fived each other.

Chapter Five

"We're taking a trip to the ATL," Takela said.

The women were at Takela's home. She called a meeting after she confirmed the details of a contract she received.

"What's in Atlanta?" Shay asked.

"The next target, of course," Kayla said sarcastically. Shay just rolled her eyes.

"We have been hired to take down an entire organization, starting with a guy named Blue. He's into a bunch of shit, like human trafficking, drug trafficking, money laundering, and much more. His name carries weight. He will not be an easy mark at all.

"To get him, we'll have to be on some undercover type of shit. The only way to take him and the entire organization, that stretches across the border, down is to be on the inside," explained Takela.

She handed each girl photos of the head men in charge, starting with Blue. One would never think a man as sexy as Blue could be so evil.

Blue stood at six feet, three inches and weighed two hundred forty pounds, all muscle, with light skin. He could go for the actor Adam Rodriguez, but Blue was finer.

His mother was Latina, and his father was Black. He grew up in a stable home, yet he turned out to be so fucked up. He was indeed a wolf in sheep's clothing.

"The client paid fifty million to get this done. He is also offering whatever resources we need to complete the job. We must do this slowly. As I stated earlier, to pull this off, we will need someone on the inside. One of us will have to go in as bait. It may take a few weeks to set everything up. This is a major hit.

"All the men you see in the photos are very powerful. Each quarter, they all meet with Blue to discuss business. Each meeting is held at a secret location known only to those who will be in attendance. From the outside, it seems that Blue has very loyal workers who would die before they cross him, so we cannot rely on any workers. This will be like a game of chess. Each move needs to be calculated and planned. It's all about strategy," Takela explained.

"So, which one of us will be on the inside?" Kayla asked.

"If no one wants to go in, I have no problem doing so," said Takela.

"Nah, we gone need you out here," Monica said.

"I will do it," Monica said.

"You sure?" Takela asked.

"Yes, I can handle it, damn. Everybody looking at me like I may fuck up," she said.

"Girl, nah. I know you are more than capable of playing your position, honey. We just shocked that you were the first to volunteer," Takela said.

"Okay. We will be leaving out on Thursday morning. We need to scope out the scene before we send you in," Takela said.

"Alright, don't be sending me on no damn suicide mission," Monica laughed.

"Bitch, you volunteered," Kayla laughed.

"So, how have things been on the home front?" Kayla asked Takela.

"Everything is straight. Mason is Mason, and I'm me," she answered.

"That doesn't really sound healthy," Shay joked, causing everyone to laugh.

"I mean, we're good. He is getting a bit too nosy for me. He wants to know every detail of every job we do. It's like he's trying to track my every move. At first, I chalked it up to him just wanting to make sure I'm okay. But now, it's like he just wants to keep tabs on me for his own selfish reasons, which is why he doesn't know about this mission. He's too much right now," she said as she took a sip of her drink.

"I hear you girl, but he may really be asking because he wants to make sure you okay. I mean, you don't have to tell him every detail of every lick, but at least tell him the basics. You'll never know when you may need him to intervene," Kayla said.

"I guess," Takela said bitterly.

"Girl, bye," said Kayla as she stood, preparing to leave.

"Just eat and leave, then," said Takela.

"Just a damn freeloader. The next meeting will be at your house, and bitch I want a whole damn feast, buffet style," said Takela.

"That trick can't cook. She gone burn her damn house down," Shay laughed.

"Damn, talk about me like I ain't here, then," Kayla said.

"Bitch, get out your feelings," Takela said, hugging her girls as they all headed out. She then started to clean up the mess they'd made. She was hoping Mason came in soon. He had become a bit over possessive , but she hadn't seen him in two days. She missed him, and she needed some dick. She grabbed her phone and dialed his number.

"What's up, my queen?" he said.

"Hey, baby. Are you coming home tonight? I miss you," she said.

"I miss you, too. I've been getting in some work. I still have some loose ends that I need to tie, then I'm coming home. Give me a few hours, baby," he said.

"Okay, baby. I'll see you when you get here. I love you," she said.

"I love you more," he said, then ended the call. He had been missing her a lot, but it was work first, play later.

Takela decided to show him how much she missed him. She found one of the many lingerie sets she had purchased online from lingeriediva.com.

He loved her in red, so she chose a red and black, rose-ruffled corset, with matching thong and thigh high stockings. She finished her look with six-inch open-toe stiletto pumps. She let her hair flow freely down her back.

She stepped out of her heels and pushed them to the side until she was ready for them. She threw on a robe and headed toward the kitchen where she fixed him a plate and waited for him. A little over an hour later, she heard his key unlock the door.

She was laying on the couch reading. He walked over kissed her, then headed straight for the kitchen like she knew he would.

Men, she said to herself, then smiled.

After heating up his plate, she made her way to the master bathroom, where she ran him a bubble bath. She had a trail of rose petals leading the way from the tub to the bed.

When she went back in the living room, he was done eating, and was ready to relieve some stress.

"You gotta wash the street sent off you first, baby. Come on," she said as she led him to the bathroom.

He smiled from ear-to-ear as she undressed him. She gave him time to soak and relax his muscles, then she entered and gave him a bath. She left out before he got out and got ready for him.

As he exited the bathroom, he followed the trail of rose petals. Takela posed as she sat on the bed. The burning candles set the mood.

She proceeded to walk toward him. Mason's mouth was wide open. He had been with her over five years, yet he still was in awe of her natural beauty. She kissed him passionately and then got on her knees.

She loosened the towel and let it fall, exposing his semi-hard dick. She licked her lips, anticipating its taste. She ran her tongue across the head of his dick slowly. She began to tongue kiss his dick.

"Sssssss," he moaned.

She lifted his dick and started sucking his balls, then running her tongue over them. She took him all in and held him there for a few seconds. She knew he loved when she did that.

She spat on the dick and sucked his dick as if her life depended on it. She deep-throated him and held him in her throat as she looked into his eyes. A tear fell from her eye as she tried to hold him a bit longer. That turned him on even more, causing him to get even harder.

She moaned as she slurped on his dick, causing the vibrations to take him over the edge. Just before she felt him about to nut, she stood.

"Damn, ma, you the best," he said as he smacked her on her ass.

"Bend over," he demanded.

She did, and he instantly went to work on her licking her ass. causing her legs to wobble.

"Damn, b-b-aby, that feels so good," she moaned.

He used his fingers to fuck her and tongue fucked her ass. His tongue was long, and he did something to make his tongue curve just right to make her squirt. She came in under three minutes, but he didn't stop there.

"Ohhh shit, baby, oh my ohhh," she moaned, trying to get away from his tongue.

He could make her cum so hard that she needed a few minutes to recuperate. He wasn't having that shit.

"Nah, don't run from me, baby. Give me my pussy. Feed me," he said as he ate her pussy and ass mercilessly.

She just knew the entire neighborhood heard her moans. After making her cum three more times, he stood.

"Stay just like that," he instructed her. She was touching her toes when he dived into her wetness, causing her to shake. They fucked for hours.

Chapter Six

That following Thursday, the ladies headed out. They decided to drive to Atlanta since it was only a few hours away. It was strictly business when they got there. Each woman had a certain part of the city to scope out. They wanted to know every street and landmark there. They went to every hood, as well as the suburbs.

It didn't take them long at all to find Blue. They learned that he pretty much ran the city. Everything that was sold came from him. Every corner boy worked for him. He owned a few lucrative businesses as well.

He had a strip club where he did most of his human trafficking. Everything under the sun went down there. It had back rooms where the ladies took the customers if they wanted more than a simple dance. He had a full drug ring going on.

They also learned that he had a lot of police on his payroll. Most of them were simply paid to turn their heads to the dealings, while others were in on the operations.

They found one of Blue's mains. Monica wasn't too thrilled to find out that all of the ladies Blue had at the strip club stayed with him, and they weren't there by choice. She wondered if he didn't have them in there under lock and key why they wouldn't leave. That was odd to her.

After doing more research, she found that neither girl left because they wouldn't make it ten feet from him. Blue ran the city with an iron fist, and damn near everyone worked for him. They all knew Blue's women, so they were fucked. They would turn them in strictly from fear of what he would do to them if they helped one of them.

Most of the women were there because they were either snatched by him or one of his henchmen after Blue saw them and claimed them. He only claimed the baddest, or they were there paying off a debt from their man or father.

He didn't buy women, but he sold them. The ones he chose to be in his home were not for sale. They could prostitute for him, but they came back after they were done. The only way he sold one of them was if they fucked up by stealing, trying to leave, or weren't bringing in money. Mostly when the pussy was dried up.

Blue had no problem fucking a bitch up, either. He would stomp a bitch damn near to death in broad daylight, with an entire crowd watching, like it was nothing. If a bitch looked at him the wrong way, she was beaten.

Monica felt like she was in way over her head, but she chose not to voice her opinion to her girls. She had volunteered, so she thought she would come off as a coward if she backed out. For this reason, she held her head high.

"You think you ready?" Takela asked her.

"Yup," she answered.

"He'll have to notice you in order to get you in. He only chooses the baddest, so you have no worries. You shitting on some of the bitches he got now, but they still bad. I set you up in an apartment close by one of his trap houses. He visits there often, but he's random, so there is no specific time he'll be there. Once he notices you, he gone want you. If I'm correct, which I think I am, he will have you before the end of the week," Takela explained.

"Okay, let's do this," she said.

As luck would have it, right after she finished getting everything together, she just happened to walk to the corner store when she saw the all-black Audi A8 with matching rims pull up across the street from her.

She was a nervous wreck. She composed herself and continued to walk. She could feel eyes on her as she passed. She heard someone, who she assumed to be Blue, ask, "Who is she?" but she didn't hear a reply.

Next, she heard, "I want her."

Got him, she said to herself as she headed for the store.

As she approached the counter to pay for her items, she noticed Blue standing in line. The picture Takela showed of him did little to no justice to him. He was F.I.N.E. She was mesmerized by his blue eyes.

"You new around here?" he asked her.

"Yeah, I just got here yesterday," she lied.

"Where you coming from?" he asked.

"Memphis," she said.

"Oh, ok," was all he said, then he left the store.

When she exited the store, she didn't see Blue anywhere, and his car was gone. She was a nervous wreck as she entered the house.

Damn, I hope I didn't fuck this up, she said to herself. *Calm down, Monica. You got this*, she said giving herself a pep talk.

She decided to finish decorating to take her mind off it.

"Gotta make it look like a home, even if I won't be long," she said.

That night, Monica heard a loud commotion coming from outside. She stepped out to see a couple fighting. They were in a full-out brawl. There was a huge crowd around them.

"Ugh," she said as she turned back around and walked back to her door. She hated the ratchet shenanigans. She locked her door and continued decorating.

She called it a night early and headed for the shower. When she finished, she stepped out, wrapped her towel around her, and went to her room. She stopped when she noticed the light in the kitchen was on.

"I could've sworn I turned that damn light off," she said.

She went to turn it back off. As she walked toward the front, she stopped in her tracks when she noticed three masked men standing in her living room. She turned to try to run to her room, only to be stopped by a fourth man at her bedroom door.

"We can do this shit the easy way, or we can do this shit the hard way. But either way, we're taking you to Blue," the guy said and laughed.

Even though Monica knew this was part of the plan, she still couldn't help feeling scared. The man snatched her and covered her nose and mouth with a piece of fabric. A few seconds later, everything went dark around her.

Chapter Seven

When Monica woke up, she was in a dark room. She was tied to the bedpost, and she was naked.

"What the fuck is this?" she asked.

She tried to see if she could maneuver her way out of the ties, but they were tied too tight. She heard a noise outside the room, and began to cry for help.

This nigga gone kill my ass. What the fuck did I get myself into? she asked herself.

The door to the room opened, and she saw a woman and a man walk in.

"I told you she was up," the woman said. The guy waved her off.

"Hey, I'm Jaz. Do you know where you are?" she asked.

Monica shook her head no.

"Look, you at Blue's house. Do you know who Blue is?" Jaz asked.

Monica shook her head no again.

"Okay. He run all this shit here. He wanted you, so he sent his men to bring you here. Since they brought you here, you won't be sold. That is if you don't fuck up and get on his bad side. You can say he holding you here as a hostage. If you try to run, trust me boo, you won't make it two feet. He will kill you before he let you go. He bought me here a few years ago. Trust me when I say there is nowhere else to go. We Blue property. We his hoes. Be smart about the situation you find yourself in. Okay, honey?" Jaz said.

"Okay," Monica responded.

"These niggas bought you in here naked, but I got you something to put on," Jaz said as she went in the drawer beside the bed. She pulled out a pair of tights and a tank top.

"I'm going to have Trae untie you. Remember what I told you earlier. Don't make a fucked up situation worse. Trae," she said motioning for him to untie her.

When he untied her, Monica rubbed her sore wrists. She grabbed the clothes and began to dress quickly. Trae watched her with this perverted look in his eyes that made her even more uncomfortable.

"What's your name?" Jaz asked.

"Monica," she answered.

"Blue is out right now, and he doesn't want you leaving this room, so I will be bringing you the necessities you need. Here is something to eat and drink. The bathroom is right there. Everything you need is in there. I'll come back to check on you in a few," Jaz said, and she and Trae exited the room.

When they left, Monica opened the tray and found spaghetti, fish, and slaw. She threw it to the side. She didn't want any food that was cooked in that house. She kept the bottled water, though.

When she went to the bathroom, she found towels, Dove soap, tissues, toothpaste, tooth brushes, and a few other hygiene supplies.

She found a small knife in the bath closet. It was a bit small, but Monica could tell it was sharp. She put it in her waistline for protection.

Three hours had passed before she heard someone at the door. She knew it was late in the evening, because when Jaz came, nightfall had just come.

She rolled over on her side with her back to the door and pretended to be fast asleep. She could see the dim light from the hall as the door was eased open.

"Is she still in here?" Monica heard one of the guys ask.

"Where the fuck else would she be, blind ass nigga? You can't see her laying right in front of you," another man responded.

"Fuck you," the man said. Monica knew it was at least three of them.

When they cut the light on, Monica counted five men total. They were shocked to see that she was awake.

"What do you want?" Monica asked.

"That pussy," one of the men answered, and they all started to laugh.

At that moment, Monica wished she hadn't volunteered. She wished she could back out now, but she knew she was already in too deep since Blue had her in his home now.

"Don't touch me," she snapped. All five men surrounded her.

"Hold this bitch down. I gotta get a taste of this fresh meat first," the guy said as he pulled his dick out and stepped out of his pants.

When they tried to hold her down, she discreetly reached into her leggings and pulled out the knife. Neither man noticed the knife until it was too late. She went for the man to her left and stuck the knife directly in his neck hitting his carotid artery, stopping him in his tracks immediately.

She went for the next guy cutting him in the exact same spot. She moved with expertise as she stuck the knife into the third man's mouth causing him to back up and scream.

"Ahhhh, you bitch!" he yelled.

By this time, the last two men were well aware of the knife. The guy that pulled his dick out tried to lunge for her, but he tripped. His pants were around his ankles causing him to lose his balance. She still managed to cut him across his face, instantly opening a gash.

She jumped out the bed and ran toward the fifth, a crazed woman. She jumped on him before he could move and started to stick him anywhere she could. She went for his neck, his arms, and his face; anywhere she could stick him.

After being stuck twice in the throat, the man fell. As she tried to get off the floor, she saw the other coming toward her in her peripheral. She ducked just in time as he tried to grab her. He caused them both to fall, but Monica was much quicker than him.

"What the hell is going on?" Monica heard a female say.

"What the fuck is this new bitch doing?" another woman said.

"Aw hell nah, Blue about to kill this bitch," one woman said, laughing.

"Check this shit out," she said.

Monica rolled over and stuck the knife in his chest, then his throat, then his chest again. She stuck him in his dick repeatedly like a raving lunatic.

"Oh my God, Monica, what did you do?" Monica heard Jaz ask her.

When she looked up, she noticed the crowd that had been drawn by the noise.

"They, they tried to hold me down and r-rape me," she said.

"Where the hell did the hoe get a knife from?" a Latina chick asked, amused.

"Damn, she fucked them niggas up," the woman standing beside Jaz said.

"Are they dead?" asked a woman that didn't look a day over sixteen.

"Obviously," answered the other woman.

Monica noticed Jaz look her way. She became scared when she noticed the fear Jaz in her eyes, as though Jaz knew Monica was about to get fucked up.

"Blue ain't here, but when he get here, there's gone be hell to pay," Jaz said.

"You still can't leave this room," Jaz said as the crowd began to disperse.

Jaz was the last to leave, leaving Monica in there with five dead bodies. She didn't attempt to clean herself up. She just got into the bed, rolled over on her side, and before she knew it, she was out.

Chapter Eight

Monica woke up to find men in the room. She noticed that the bodies were gone. The men in the room appeared to be cleaning up. She had always been a light sleeper. She could hear a pin drop in her sleep, yet she didn't hear the men come and remove the bodies.

She looked around and noticed the knife she had put on the dresser was gone. When one of the men looked up and saw that she was up, he hurriedly left the room. A few minutes later, he came back with two other men.

"Have anyone of y'all talked to Blue?" one of the men asked.

"Yeah, he knows and is on his way," he answered.

They just stood in the doorway and stared at her.

"Blue is here," someone yelled.

Monica's hands began to sweat. At first, she was nervous. But fear took over when she started to wonder what he would do to her. The look in Jaz's eyes scared her even more.

Moments later, she saw the infamous Blue standing in the doorway, glaring at her. She couldn't read his expression. In fact, she saw nothing when she looked at him. This scared her more than anything, but she refused to show it. She held her own poker face.

Blue instructed the man to his right, Jack, to grab her. Monica got into her fighting stance and prepared to fight until there was no fight left in her. At that moment, she wasn't thinking about the job or the fifty million they were being paid when the job was over. She was thinking about survival.

The man reached forward as if he was about to snatch her by her arm, but instead, he ducked and snatched her ankle, causing her to lose her balance. She anticipated him grabbing her arm, so when he didn't, she couldn't respond like she wanted to. He pulled her out the bed and dragged her like she was a rag doll. She went kicking and screaming.

He started to lose his grip around her ankle, so he tried to reach for her other ankle, but was met with a knee to his groin so fierce that he stopped in his tracks and knelt down in pain.

"Bitch!" he yelled. Then she saw the other man coming for her. She reached for the dresser drawer and pulled it out. Just as he was within arm's reach, she swung the dresser connecting with his jaw.

"Fuck!" he said as he hit her, knocking her to the ground.

"Fuck is wrong with you soft ass niggas?" Blue asked rhetorically.

He snatched Monica by her hair with a firm grip. He dragged her out the room, down the long hallway, and up another flight of steps that lead an entire floor that was considered his workout area. He had all the latest equipment in there.

He opened the bathroom door where there was only a shower and threw her in as if she weighed two pounds. Her head hit the floor with a loud thud. She passed out.

The cold water from the shower woke her up. The water felt as though she was being stabbed with sharp daggers everywhere.

"Ahhhh!" she screamed out.

She noticed Blue standing over her, spraying her. She looked down and noticed she was naked. She also noticed the ice around her and the bucket it came from sitting on the side of Blue.

She couldn't keep cool this time. She screamed as Blue continued to spray her. He snatched her by her hair and dumped her head in the bucket of ice water. She instantly began to gag and choke. He let her up, slapped her, then dumped her head back in the bucket.

"Bitch, you actually had the fucking nerve to not stab and kill one of my men, but five," he said as he repeatedly slapped her and held her down on the bucket until she almost passed out.

Her face was swollen. Had Blue not been trying to drown her, her face would've been bloodied as well. He then dumped what appeared to be warm soapy water on her and pulled her out the shower by her hair.

Monica no longer fought or screamed, she just allowed him to drag her in her zombie-like state. He tied her to a pole in the center of the room and left her there, naked.

Chapter Nine

While Monica was working on the inside, her girls were working as well. It wasn't hard to figure out who the HNICs were. Just in case Monica being on the inside didn't work out, they went to Plan B.

Shay went for one of Blue's head henchmen named Calli. He was known for his murder game. That, and his loyalty, made him rise to Blue's side in record time. Blue wasn't a man who trusted easily, but Calli proved his loyalty on numerous occasions. Now, he was one of Blue's right-hand men. Shay knew she could bait him in.

Like Monica, Shay knew she had to move slowly. A man of his caliber could sniff her out miles away. She had to play her cards smart. A losing hand didn't mean you couldn't win the game. It was all about how you played the hand you were dealt, and Shay was playing for keeps.

She decided to rent a house on the other side of town. She knew niggas of his caliber rarely went for a hood chick. It was always the opposite. She also didn't want to settle for a place in the hood, because she didn't want anyone there to know her or remember her. She preferred to move in silence.

She found out that Calli was a regular customer at Starbucks. He was there every morning at the same time.

"Somebody should've told him that schedules are deadly. He is making himself an easy target. Always move randomly," said Shay.

"You would think he would be a tad bit smarter," Takela added

"I guess he just know a nigga ain't stupid enough to try him," Kayla said.

While Shay chose to bait Calli, Kayla chose to go for another one of Blue's head henchmen, Quan. Not only was Quan one of Blue's top henchmen, but he was also Blue's best friend. They'd been friends since the sandbox. They were as close as brothers.

Like Shay, Kayla rented a small two-bedroom house away from the hood. She chose a quiet suburban area with an extremely low crime rate.

Kayla found out about an all-white affair that was being thrown, and Quan would be in attendance. As she prepared for the affair, Shay was on the other side of town parked outside of Starbucks awaiting Calli's arrival. She didn't want to go in before him and risk him not noticing her. She knew it wouldn't be a smart of her to approach him. All she had to do was walk in, and the rest would be smooth sailing. She was bad, and she knew it. Shay knew he would be on her jock.

Shay noticed an all-black 2017 Cadillac CTS pull into the lot. She instantly knew it was Calli. When he stepped out, Shay was in awe of how fine he was.

"Damn, this nigga fine as fuck," she said.

Shay had seen him quite a few times, but never up close. She was damn near drooling at the mouth.

Calli had a caramel complexion. He stood at six feet, one inch and weighed two-hundred and fifty pounds; all muscle. He had honey-colored, bedroom eyes, full lips, and perfect white teeth. He had tattoos covering both arms. He resembled Shamar Moore.

Damn, Shay, get it together, she told herself as she composed herself.

She knew he wouldn't be in there very long, so she needed to move fast. On a normal morning, the longest he would be there was about 10-15 minutes, at best. She waited five minutes after he went in to exit her car.

It was mid-September. Fall was underway, and most were cherishing the last of the heat, but it was at its minimum. Shay wore a Valentino lace yoke half-sleeve tan dress with some Christian Louboutin Madcarina knotted tan wedges.

As she walked in, she caught the eyes of men and women. Some, of course, were hating, while others were admiring her beauty. She walked toward the counter to place her order. She noticed Calli was standing to the side, and assumed he was waiting for his order to be filled.

A few guys tried to holla, but she brushed them off nicely. Calli saw her when she came in, but he wasn't one to be all on a chick. If he wanted her, he would approach her, and if not, he kept pushing. He was among the rare few that didn't allow pussy to fuck up his flow. He admitted to himself that she was bad as fuck, though. He wanted to feel her out first. He was good at reading people.

After Shay had gotten her order, she noticed Calli still in the shop. He was seated at one of the tables in the front, going through his phone. Her pride was a bit wounded when she noticed he wasn't going to approach her. She headed out the door. Just as she unlocked her car, she heard someone call out.

"Excuse me."

She turned in her tracks to see Calli. She hoped the relief she felt when she turned around didn't show on her face.

"What's up?" she asked.

"You got a man, ma?" he asked getting right to the point.

"Um, no. I prefer the single route," she said.

"That's what's up. I like what I see and would like to get to know you, if you don't mind," he said.

She nodded.

"Take this phone. I'll call you later," he said, handing her an iPhone. He walked toward his car, got in, and left.

"Well damn," she said as she got into her car and left as well.

Chapter Ten

Kayla gave herself a once over in the mirror. For the affair, she chose an Alexander McQueen crisscross front woodgrain metallic white mini-dress with matching stilettos. She decided to wear an up do. She knew she would grab the attention of every man and chick in the building.

"Alright, let's get it," she said as she headed toward her all-white Lexus LS.

The affair was being hosted on a beautiful yacht. The setup was immaculate. She had no problem easing onto the yacht with no invite. She mingled around and downed a few glasses of champagne. Right before the yacht was about to set sail, she noticed Quan and his entourage board. Quan could easily be spotted as he entered.

He was mixed with Black and Latino. He was six feet, one inch with curly hair that he wore brushed back in a ponytail. He was light-skinned with a panty-dropping smile. He, too, was tatted up. He didn't wear his clothes hanging off him like most hood niggas.

Kayla knew she could get lost in him and his sexiness, if she wasn't careful. He just had this heartbreaker demeanor going on. She chose to stand on the sideline, looking at the waves as she sipped from her cup.

As she admired the waves, she felt a hand on her lower back.

"Hello, beautiful," Quan said.

"Hello. You don't look bad yourself," she said smiling.

"Why are you standing alone? Why not join the party?" he said as he waved his hand around him. Most of the partygoers were either dancing or entertaining, yet she was over there alone.

"Just admiring the waves. It amazes me how something so beautiful could be so deadly," she said, not taking her eyes off the water.

"Yeah, me too. Just like fire. I'm Quan, and you are?" he asked.

"Nice to meet you, Quan. I'm Kayla," she said, not meaning to give her real name. She wanted to kick herself for that amateur move.

"Kayla," Quan repeated.

Before either of the realized it, the party was just about over. They'd spent the last two and a half hours talking and chilling. A woman had never been able to keep Quan's attention for more than a few minutes, let alone over two hours. He really enjoyed her company, and he didn't want the night to end.

There were only a few guests still mingling around. The liquor had Kayla feeling bold. She found Quan's lips to be irresistible. She placed her hand on the back of his neck, pulled his head down, and gave him a passionate kiss. He could taste the remnants of the champagne she had consumed not long ago.

She slowly sucked his bottom lip. She could feel him rise in his pants. She wanted him. Right there.

Quan became a little more aggressive with the kiss, turning her on even more. He pulled her closer to him and grabbed her ass. He proceeded to kiss her neck, causing her panties to become drenched. When he started to suck on her neck, she was lost in him. She reached for his pants, wanting him inside her right then.

"Fuck me," she said as she looked in his eyes.

Quan lifted her onto the rail of the boat. He lifted her dress and slid her thong to the side. When she released him from his jeans, her mouth fell open even before she could see his length. She felt it and knew he could do some major damage, which is exactly what she wanted.

He was used to women gasping at his length. He rubbed his head over her opening, wetting his dick. She was drenched, and he loved it. He bit down on her neck to lighten the blow as he inserted his full, thick, ten inches inside her wetness, causing her body to jump.

"Ohhhh," she moaned as he moved slowly inside her. As he fucked her slowly, he removed one of her breasts from her dress and bit down on her nipple gently.

"Sssssss, you feel so good. Yessss," she moaned out as he sped up his pace.

"Oh, fuck, right there. Yes, right there, baby. Fuck me," she moaned.

He began to fuck her hard, causing her to shake each time he hit bottom.

"Damn, ma," he said as she became wetter and wetter the harder he went.

"Oh my! Fuck, Quan, right there. Oh, yes, make me cum baby," she moaned out as he hit her spot.

"Ohhh, Q-Q-Q-Quan," she screamed out as she came all over his dick.

He lifted her from the rail, still inside her, and carried her to the first room on the yacht where they fucked themselves into a deep sleep.

Chapter Eleven

"Hey, girl, wake up. Monica? Monica?" Jaz said as she shook Monica awake.

Monica had spent the entire day up there. She was hungry, tired, and in pain.

"Hey, get up," Jaz said.

Monica didn't know where she was for a moment, then it all came back to her.

"Hey, I bought you something to put on and something to eat," Jaz said.

"Girl, the only way you gone survive here is if you get with the program and play your position. Shit, I don't want to be here either, but right now I have no choice," Jaz said.

"How can someone get used to this? How can you live under these conditions?" Monica asked.

"It's called survival, honey. You will never be able to get used to this. You'll never be able to get comfortable with this, but you need to learn to adjust to this. This is where you are, and right now there is nothing you can do about it. Don't get yourself killed. Let your survival instincts kick in. Trust me, I've seen chicks come in here just like you. Ready to fight their way out of here. The ones that come in like that don't last very long. Blue will not hesitate to kill you. All I'm saying is, be smart about the situation. Survive, baby girl," Jaz said as she helped Monica into the clothes.

Monica took everything she said into consideration. Jaz fed her the food she brought up and left shortly afterwards.

"I can't stay any longer because Blue wants me down at the club tonight. I will check on you first thing tomorrow morning," Jaz said as she departed, leaving Monica feeling stuck.

These bitches in here are crazy, Monica said to herself. *Ain't no fucking way I would just take this lying down. That nigga would have to kill me*, she said.

Later the next evening, Monica heard footsteps coming up the stairs. Three men came into the room. Those fools actually had on gloves and even went as far as to have on what looked to be a safety vest. She began to laugh at them.

"I guess y'all came prepared this time," she said still laughing.

"Brah, this bitch crazy. I think Blue has met his match with this one," one of the men said.

"Look, we not trying to take it there with you, alright? Blue sent us to bring you to him, and that's it, ma. Save all that crazy shit for him, alright?" he said.

One of the men grabbed her by her foot the other one grabbed her wrist and held her as the last man untied her.

"Alright," one said after they untied her.

Monica followed them down the steps and toward the main entrance of the mansion. They stopped in front of the kitchen where

Monica recognized Blue standing in front of the sink. He looked as if he'd just stepped off the cover of GQ Magazine.

This nigga is just too fine, she thought.

"I hope he fuck this bitch up for killing my nigga," she heard the man to her right whisper.

She looked back at him to see him mugging her hard. He had a hateful glare in his eyes that she knew would become an issue if she didn't handle it. She saw the Chinese chef butcher knife lying on the counter and went for it.

Before anyone could react, she had the knife in his throat attempting to decapitate him. Had they not snatched her, she might have succeeded.

"What the fuck?!" Blue yelled as he watched the mayhem.

"I told you this bitch crazy," one of the men said as he tried his best to knock the air out of Monica's lungs, but she kept fighting.

The other women in the house watched. Some in complete horror, and others were amused at how much chaos one woman had caused in forty-eight hours. This was the sixth man she had killed in her short stay. Most were wondering why Blue hadn't ended her yet. They'd seen him end bitches' lives for much less, yet Monica was still breathing. His top hoes were all jealous.

"Fuck this bitch still breathing for?" one of his top hoes, Tasha, let slip from her mouth.

She didn't realize she said the shit out loud, until Blue gave her a deadly gaze, causing her to back up.

"Move!" Blue yelled as he snatched Monica.

"Aw yea, that bitch crazy," another hoe, Chell, said as she watched in disbelief as Monica had the nerve to swing at Blue.

Blue delivered a smack so fierce that it halted her next swing, but only for a second. She swung at him again, this time connecting with the left side of his face. He snatched her by her hair and dragged her up the stairs toward his room.

"Damn, she gone get herself killed," Jaz said as she watched the interaction in disbelief.

Chapter Twelve

"Where the fuck are you, Takela?" Mason asked.

"Me and the ladies are in Florida. We won't be too long," Takela lied.

She refused to tell him where they were. Mason had been trying to get her to stop taking contracts. He figured that she needed to get out while she could, because karma would come showing her face at any moment. The last thing he wanted was for him or her to be face to face with karma.

"Don't lie to me, ma," Mason said, his tone softening.

Takela hated to lie to him, but she had made up her mind that this would be the last contract she would take. She had more than enough money. She just didn't want to tell him where she really was, because she couldn't afford any errors on this contract. The money for this hit was what she needed to retire from it all. She hadn't talked to her girls about retiring, but she planned to do so after this assignment.

"Baby, I'm not lying to you. We should be finished here by Friday, then I'm throwing the towel in, and coming home to you, baby. I promise," she said, trying to convince him.

"Alright, ma," he said, knowing she was lying. There was nothing he could do.

"Okay, baby, I have to go, but I will call you in the morning. Love you, baby. Goodnight," she said.

"Love you too, baby. Goodnight," Mason said as he ended the call.

Takela decided to play the background in the entire setup. She chose to stay hidden. She was working on finding a way to contact Monica from the inside.

She knew that after a few days there, Blue had each lady do a debut in the strip club. She assumed it wouldn't be long before Monica would show up, so she waited.

She'd visited the club twice and found that, although it looked like a hole in the wall on the outside, it was beautiful and spacious inside. She could tell a professional decorated the club.

The club entire stage and the poles were made of glass, so was the bar. There were three floors. Of course, the higher the floor, the higher your status. There were three offices inside the club. One was hidden on the third floor. No one knew it was there. It looked as though it was just a wall, but Takela knew better. She hadn't gotten this far by being basic.

She made sure to dress down when visiting the club. With her looks, she knew she would be a target for Blue, so she hid most of her beauty and her body. She decided to go in dressed as a stud. She knew a stud wouldn't draw any negative attention.

The first time she went in, she chose to sit in the back and observed the club's layout. She paid for a lap dance so she could blend in with the other patrons. She noticed that all of the dancers looked like supermodels, but the best dancers, of course, were in VIP.

The second time she entered the club, she paid the VIP fee for the second floor. There, she finally made a little progress where Monica was concerned. As she entered the VIP area, she immediately went to her table and paid for a lap dance. She noticed the young lady looked as if something heavy was on her mind, so she decided to strike up a conversation with her. At first, the dancer acted as if she wasn't interested in speaking with her. She appeared to be uncomfortable.

"Is there anything I can do to make you feel a little more comfortable?" Takela asked the dancer.

The dancer realized she was acting a bit rude, so she changed her attitude. She just wasn't in it.

"I'm sorry. No, you're fine," she said.

"What's your name?" Takela asked.

At first, she appeared as if she wasn't comfortable answering her, but then she threw caution to the wind.

"I'm Jaz, and you are?" Jaz said as she danced.

"Nice to meet you Jaz, I'm Tee," Takela answered.

"Likewise," Jaz said.

"You live around here?' Takela asked.

"Um, no. I, um, I live with my um, my man," Jaz stammered.

"Oh, ok," said Takela.

"I don't live around here, either. I came looking for my friend. She came here one night with some guy she met at the hotel we were staying at, but I haven't seen her since," Takela said.

She felt like no harm could come from saying she was simply looking for a friend. Besides, she wasn't revealing any information.

Jaz's ears perked up when Takela mentioned she was looking for her friend.

"What's your friend's name?" Jaz asked.

"Her name is Monica. She is about five-five or five-six, probably weighs about a hundred forty pounds. She has a caramel complexion with a tattoo of her zodiac sign on her wrist," she continued.

"Sorry, I have to go," Jaz said suddenly as the song ended

"Okay, sure. Thanks," Takela said as Jaz walked off.

Takela knew Jaz would be a good asset to have. She had always been able to read a chick and pick out the loyal ones, most times before they opened their mouths. She knew going around looking for Monica was risky and wasn't part of the plan, but she had a feeling Jaz would be of much assistance.

Chapter Thirteen

Bbrrrring. Bbrrrring. Was the sound that woke Shay from her peaceful sleep.

She rolled over, looking for phone. As she reached it, she noticed the screen was still dark, but she still heard ringing. The sound was coming from her purse. As she reached in her purse, she instantly perked up, noticing the phone Calli gave her was ringing.

"Hello," she answered, trying not to sound as happy as she really was to hear from him.

"Hey, ma. What you got going?" Calli asked.

"Well, I was sleep until I was rudely interrupted," she said.

"Oh, sorry to hear that. Tell whatever nigga interrupted your beauty sleep to get a fucking life," he said as if it wasn't him. "Anyway," he continued. "I want to take you to breakfast in the morning, say around eight," he said.

"You mean in four hours," she said as she looked at the clock.

"Yeah. You game?" he asked.

"I guess."

"Don't guess, ma. Are you game?" he asked again.

"Of course," she answered.

"That's more like it," he said, sounding cocky.

"And where are we meeting?" she asked.

"The Café. It's located in The Ritz Carlton on Peachtree. Do you know where that is?"

"My GPS does," she answered. He laughed.

Women, he thought to himself.

"Alright, ma. Meet me there at eight."

"Will do," she said.

They both ended the call.

Shay knew it was going to be extremely hard to go back to sleep. She was too anxious to see what the next day would bring. She knew it wouldn't be the brightest idea to stay up, so she popped a Unisom and was asleep before she knew it.

She woke up at 6:30 the next morning, regretting taking the pill. She felt so drowsy, and drank a cup of coffee to fight off the effect of the drug. She chose to dress down that particular morning. She knew she had already baited him and didn't want to overdo it. She wore a pair of stretch jeans that hugged her curves, a black tank top, chic diamond encrusted body chain, and some black wedges. She let her hair hang with loose curls, did her usual once over in the mirror, then she headed out the door. It took her no time to make it to The Café. She dialed the number back that Calli called from.

"I see you. I've already been seated. You'll see me sitting to your left when you come in," he said, before she said hello.

"Okay," was all she said as she walked toward the door.

Calli admired Shay from afar. He saw her when she first pulled in. She was sexy as hell to him. He could tell she was from the south, but knew she wasn't from Atlanta. That was a plus in his book. He wasn't trying to entertain another basic chick from the ATL.

Dealing with hood chicks always made him feel out of his element. He normally met them at the club, and couldn't remember them by the crack of dawn. He stood as she approached and pulled her chair out.

"Good morning, early bird," she said as she sat down.

"The early bird-, you know the saying. Good morning." he said as he took a seat after her.

They both placed their orders and made small talk until their orders came.

"So, where exactly are you from?" Calli asked.

"Wow, is it that obvious. I'm from Texas," she lied.

"What brings you to Atlanta?"

"A change in scenery. I just wanted to get away and start over. Family issues. Things weren't the same after my mom passed away. I just wanted to leave," she said, only partially lying.

Her mom did pass a few years ago, leaving a huge void in her heart. There wasn't a day that went by when she didn't think about or miss her mother.

"So, how is ATL treating you?" Calli asked, trying to lighten the mood.

"Fantastic so far. I'm looking forward to what surprises the future has in store for me," she said with a huge smile on her face and winked at him.

The two spent the morning getting to know each other. Calli liked Shay. She wasn't the typical female. He could use a woman like her on his team.

They didn't leave The Café until a little before ten, with plans to hook up the following Friday for dinner and a movie. Afterward, they both parted ways. Shay, to check the status of Takela and Kayla, and Calli headed to a pick-up with his new connect.

Chapter Fourteen

Monica hit her head on just about every step leading to Blue's bedroom. Blue tossed her across the room as if she was a rag doll. Monica landed on her side. When she saw Blue coming toward her, she instantly jumped up. Just as he reached her, she delivered a slap to the right side of his face. The slap didn't faze him as much as Monica's nerve did. He couldn't believe this bitch had actually slapped him. He slapped her back, then punched her in her side. She was still coming unruffled by his blows.

Normally, Blue would've had her brains splattered all over the floor, but what Monica was doing wasn't pissing him off. It was making his dick hard. He had never met a woman who didn't lower her eyes when in the situation Monica was in. He wasn't used to a woman fighting him back tooth and nail. She could pass one and take one twice as hard, and still stand her ground. Not to mention, behind the few bruises she had obtained while there, she was drop dead beautiful. Even with the bruises, her beauty was still present.

When she stood in a fighting stance, biting her lip, ready to go at it, he knew he had a keeper.

He ran at her and snatched her by her throat, but he lost his grip as she wiggled free from him. She then bit down as hard as she could on his arm. He slapped her again and snatched her by her hair.

He noticed that snatching her hair slowed her down. Even if only for a few seconds, that's all he needed.

He bent her over the dresser and smacked her again, not releasing the grip he had on her hair. She tried to swing at him, but she couldn't put up any resistance in the position he had her in. He snatched the shorts off her like they were paper. She continued to try to fight him off as he stepped out his jeans.

"I know what will tame you," he said he rubbed his hand over her opening to feel her wetness.

Monica couldn't help but be turned on. She had always loved the rough shit. No, she had never had a man be that rough with her, but she loved it all the same. Her pussy got even wetter anticipating Blue's fine ass sliding his dick in her.

"I'm finna give you what you want," he said, then he plunged inside of her with so much force that she stopped fighting him off completely.

"Um," she moaned.

"So this is what you wanted," he said as he began to fuck her roughly.

"Ohhhh ummmm," Monica moaned out. She was dripping wet.

"Ahhhh," Blue moaned out. Monica's pussy was so wet and so tight. This was the best pussy he had been in, by far.

"Ohhhh fuck. Fuck me!" Monica yelled out. Blue was hitting spots she didn't know she had. "Shit y-y-you're in. Ohhh t-t-that's my my," she moaned out.

"Your spot," he said as he fucked her harder.

"Fuck yesssss, ohhhhh," she moaned

"I'm cummminnng, fuckkk," she moaned out as Blue felt her squirt all over his dick.

She came so hard she pushed his dick out without even trying.

Blue led her to the bed.

"Ride this dick," he instructed her.

He didn't have to tell her twice. She climbed on top of him and slid down on his dick slowly. She lifted up on his dick, only leaving the head inside. She used her walls to grip his head as she slid up and down.

"Damn, ma," Blue said as he watched her.

He could see his dick glistening with her wetness as she rose up.

This bitch gone have me crazy, he thought as he watched her slide into a split and ride him until she squirted all over him and his bed.

It took everything in him not to nut. He knew if he kept her on top he wouldn't last much longer, so he switched positions, putting her on the bottom.

He lifted both of her legs and massaged her clit as he entered her. He hadn't taken the time to actually please a woman in the eight years since his wife. He only fucked for his benefit, and couldn't give two fucks if a bitch came or not. He just sampled her before he put her ass on the market.

Monica, on the other hand, she was different. Her pussy was different. She was different. Coming from a man who'd had a woman from all walks of life, Monica was the deal breaker. Blue went as deep as he could, then came out slowly. He fucked her like that, driving her crazy. She looked up at him.

"I want you to fuck me hard," she said.

"Like that?" he asked as he slammed into her.

"Harder," she moaned out.

Blue slammed into her even harder.

"Just. Like. That," she moaned as he fucked her.

"Ohhhh, Blue, you gone make me cum all over this dick, fffuuukkkk," she moaned.

He could tell she was close to her peak by how her walls started to tighten as he fucked her.

"Ahhhh fuuukkk," he moaned out about to cum, too.

"Just like that, baby, please don't stop," she moaned. He was on her spot. "Ohhhhh, Blue, I'm cummmmmminngg!!" she yelled.

The intensity of her orgasm caused him to cum seconds after her. Before either of them knew anything, they'd drifted to sleep.

Outside the room, the ladies were shocked. They had never seen Blue react like that with a bitch. Blue didn't realize he'd left his room door wide open for the other women to hear and peek in his room to see what was going on. Tasha, one of his top hoes, was beyond pissed.

"How this bitch gone come in here and just take the fuck over. How daddy let that bitch hit him like that, then go fuck this bitch and make sure she enjoyed the shit," she said pissed.

"I know, right," Chell said. "Who is this bitch, anyway?" Chell asked.

Unbeknownst to Monica, she had made some deadly enemies.

"Now, that's a bitch that knows how to play her position to the fullest," Jaz said as she went to her room.

She just hoped Monica would use this as an opportunity to make an escape. She had seen men like Blue before. They could easily bait a woman and have her doing the unthinkable, all for the sake of false love and good dick.

Chapter Fifteen

Kayla and Quan had been kicking it heavy. It had only been a few days. Kayla had to admit that she really enjoyed Quan's company.

Back home, she had Rocky, but he wasn't the man she needed him to be. Yes, he took care of her and her body, but mentally he was slacking. It's like he felt he could buy her. She hated that. Then, they completely stopped going out. He would only call her late nights for a booty call, then he would be gone when she awoke the next morning. She had been seeing him for over a year.

She knew she and Quan could never be. That was fine with her, but she was going to enjoy what they had until the end. He was nothing more than a job to her.

After meeting him on the yacht, she went back to his home, where they finished what they'd started. She'd allowed him to come to her home a few times as well. She told him she wanted to become a published author, and that she was working on her first series. She also told him that she was a full-time student. Everything was going well on her end.

Quan was feeling her as well. He was captivated by her beauty. He wasn't big on relationships. He had met some decent women, but after a few nights, if not after the first night, he would move on without a backward glance. He had never been in an actual relationship, and wasn't looking for one.

He liked what he saw in Kayla. She was beautiful, bold, and intellectual. She had this tough demeanor, but he could tell on the inside she was as soft as a cotton ball.

"I gotta go handle something," Quan told Kayla.

"Okay, babe," she said as she began to dry her body.

"I'll get up with you in a few days, ma," he said as he put his shirt on and grabbed his keys.

He kissed her and left. Kayla knew it would only be a matter of minutes before Quan walked back through the door to get his phone. She moved quickly as she removed the back from his phone and inserted the listening device on the back of the battery.

She saw him exit his car as she rushed to power his phone back on. She noticed her front door was still unlocked as he approached.

"Kayla," he called out as he entered the living room.

"Yeah," she answered.

"I left my phone," he said as he made his way toward the hall bath where Kayla pretended to be wrapping her hair.

"You forgot your lifeline? Never do that," she winked as she watched him go into the bedroom and retrieve his phone from the dresser.

"I normally don't," he said as he headed back for the door.

"Whew," she said. Kayla had also placed a listening device in his home office and a GPS tracker on his car.

"What's up?" Quan said into his car's Bluetooth system.

"A meeting has been called. Blue wants us at the spot in an hour," the caller said.

"Aight," Quan said as he ended the call.

He knew shit just got real. Niggas were stealing and snitching. Niggas were too greedy. Quan hated a greedy ass nigga. Blue made sure everyone on his team ate lovely. He was a fair boss, and made sure to treat all his workers equally. There weren't too many bosses that paid their workers fifty percent of the profit they brought in.

Quan pulled into the parking lot of the meeting spot, which was located in a vacant warehouse. He noticed Blue's and Calli's cars there. Blue met him at the door.

"What's good?" Blue said as they shook up.

"That's what I'm trying to find out. These niggas still clowning?" Quan asked.

"Time to clean house," Blue said.

Blue was sick of these so-called loyal niggas. Niggas didn't know the true definition of loyalty. Niggas didn't know how not to steal or snitch, for that matter.

"So who?" Calli asked.

"The Linx twins and Jake. These niggas call themselves stealing, then setting Joe and Omar up. Niggas wasn't smart at all. It's a few unknown cats too, but I plan on finding out soon. I'm gone let these niggas think everything gravy. They'll slip up. Bitch niggas always do," Blue said. He hated for a nigga to try to make a fool of him.

"Damn," Quan said. He liked the Linx twins. They were the best killers on the squad. They showed no fear.

"Aight, let's get it," Quan said, ready to do what needed to be done.

Chapter Sixteen

"Have you guys made any progress?" Takela asked Kayla and Shay.

"Yup," Kayla answered. "I was able to install the listening devices as well as the GPS. When Blue moves, so does Quan, so we'll be able to track them. So far, it appears as if Blue has a few rotten apples in the bunch. You know the usual greedy niggas that are never satisfied," Kayla answered.

"It's pretty much the same here," Shay said.

"I haven't been able to put the GPS on him yet, but it will be in place tonight. Calli is one of those men that you have to work slowly. I can tell he doesn't trust easily. He gives me the impression that he has been crossed by a woman before, so I'm moving slowly. Have you been able to get word on Monica yet?" Shay asked, worried about her girl. Monica had been there a few days with no word.

"I may have found a possible ally on the inside," Takela said.

"Who? Are you sure? They won't snitch Monica out, will they? Do you think you can trust her? Him?" Shay asked, firing question after question, not allowing Takela time to answer.

"Hold up, ma. Pump ya brakes," Takela said. "I said may have, meaning I'm not 100% sure yet. I have a feeling she's good people and isn't like that. I know she's game, even though she didn't give much info. The fact that I was able to walk out of the club afterwards let me know she's straight," she said.

"You are way too trusting for me," Kayla said.

She didn't doubt her girl one bit, but she still was cautious. When in their line of business, one couldn't afford not to be. She knew Takela had it, so she didn't protest. Shay, on the other hand, wasn't game.

"Takela, if this doesn't go right, you could get Monica killed. You can't risk that. Letting this bitch in could backfire. What the hell made you go to the club asking questions like that anyway? Asking the right person could've gotten ya ass toe tagged. You can't take risks like that, neither can you put Monica at risk like that. Remember, she's the one on the inside," Shay said, pissed off.

"Calm down, Shay, damn. I didn't get this far from being stupid. Hell, we didn't get this far from being stupid, either. I'm not a damn fool. Damn, you have no faith in me, I see. I know what the fuck I'm doing. I didn't go in like a damn lost puppy. Like I said, I know what the fuck I'm doing, just make sure you handle your end," Takela said.

Shay stormed out, pissed. Her main concern was Monica getting out of there alive. She wasn't feeling the entire plan.

Ain't no telling what they doing to her, Shay thought. She just wanted the shit to be over with.

"You and your intuitions, I hope you're right," Kayla said.

She was never one to question Takela's moves, because so far she hadn't fucked up. She always read them right.

Takela planned to visit the club again in a week. She didn't want to appear desperate. She wanted to let Jaz think on it and come to her. She had a Plan C, just in case nothing panned out. *Pray for the best, but prepare for the worst,* she thought.

"So far, it's just a waiting game," Takela said.

"I think we should hit some of Blue's trap spots," Kayla suggested.

Unbeknownst to her girls, Takela had devised a personal plan.

She wanted to start eliminating some of smaller players working under Blue. She wanted to weaken his army. She knew that Blue wouldn't reschedule the meeting because he was having issues on his Homefront, that would make him appear weak and incapable of leading the Atlanta jurisdiction. Why not shake things up a bit because she was bored with the wait?

She felt like a sitting duck. She also felt that if she made the men vulnerable, it would be easier for her girls to work their magic. She'd already been following his workers, learning about them.

Takela didn't want to let her girls in on the plan, because she knew they would object. She knew they would think she was jeopardizing all their work, so she moved in silence. She had to admit, Kayla's suggestion was much better and easier. They would be able to double the financial gain.

"Sounds good. I've been watching a few of the workers. I know where three of their trap spots is. I've also located the warehouse where he sells some of the women, as well," said Takela.

Kayla looked at her with a raised eyebrow.

"What bitch? Y'all bitches ain't the only ones that's been working. You know I ain't one to sit and wait," she joked.

"Yeah, I know, with your impatient ass," Kayla laughed.

"We can hit one of them tonight," Takela suggested.

"How when Shay will be with Calli tonight? You know we can't afford to reschedule," Kayla said.

"Me and you are more than capable of pulling it off. One of the traps only have four workers there. They are some young cats who still has milk on their tongues. They always have some silly ass little girls in there giving it up. This will be a piece of cake," Takela said.

They already had the fire power needed to pull off the hit, they just needed the attire. Kayla hopped in the car with Takela as they headed to the nearest Walmart Super Center to get the supplies needed.

Chapter Seventeen

Shay was anxious and nervous at the same time. She was looking forward to hooking up with Calli. He was supposed to be picking her up from her house.

"Fuck," she said as she looked at the clock.

He was due to be there in twenty minutes, and she was fresh out the shower, still wrapped in a towel. If that wasn't bad enough, she couldn't decide on what to wear for the evening.

She hadn't been to the movies in years. She was fifteen and chose to go with a big-headed ass boy who got mad and left her in the theater when she wouldn't give him head in the back row.

Fall was fast approaching. She opted to wear a pair of white Mathias velvet skinny jeans, a pink Majestic Paris soft touch mid-sleeve V-neck tee, a matching pink Vegan Leather moto jacket and a pair of Pink UGG Classic short crystal suede boots.

As she made a final decision on what to wear, she heard her doorbell.

"Shit," she said as she put on her robe and went to the door.

"Hi," she said, her nerves getting the best of her.

"Hey, beautiful," Calli said as he handed her a dozen beautiful red roses.

"Thanks, these are gorgeous. Give me about ten minutes. Make yourself at home. Would you like something to drink while you wait?" she asked rambling.

"No. I'm good," he said.

She scurried back to her room to finish getting dressed.

While he was waiting, Calli looked around her home. It was a lot smaller than his, but it was still a nice place. He admired her décor and noticed the odd colors she chose to pair up. She brought them out nicely.

"I'm ready," she said as she rounded the corner.

Calli couldn't help but stare. Only a woman as beautiful as her could make something so basic look so lavish.

Shay set her alarm, locked up, and headed to Calli's Cadillac.

He opened her door for her, then made sure she was secure before he walked over to the driver's side, got in the car, and drove off.

Shay busied herself with the radio trying to find something to listen to. Just about every station was on commercials, so she plugged her phone in. She went to Rihanna's new album, *Anti* and pressed play. Calli just went with it.

"So, what are we seeing tonight?" she asked him.

"*Suicide Squad*," he answered.

"Never heard of it," she admitted.

"Really? They show a preview every other commercial on TV, and they keep running the preview on the radio," Calli said.

"Well, I'm not much of a commercial woman."

"And what does that mean, ma?" he asked laughing.

"It means if it has commercials, I don't watch it. If it plays commercials, I don't listen to it. I hate sitting through commercials, especially when it's a good show or movie. It's like every time they get to the good part, a commercial interrupts you. I'm more of a premium channel and DVR kind of gal," she said and winked.

"Well damn. You miss a lot, then," he said smiling.

"Not really. Besides, if it's important, then nine times out of ten, I'll hear it," she said.

They pulled into the theater, found a parking spot, and proceeded to the ticket counter.

Just like every other Saturday, the theater was packed. There were mostly young couples and a few bad ass teens hanging around. After they'd purchased their tickets, they got popcorn and drinks, and headed in.

After the movie was over, they left the movies hand in hand.

"That was a good movie," Shay complimented.

"Yeah, I knew it would be," Calli said.

Shay's stomach began to growl as they were leaving.

"Why didn't you tell me you were hungry? We could've stop to eat before the movie."

"No, I'm fine. It was my dumb choice not to eat anything earlier so I wouldn't lose my appetite."

"Don't tell me you one of those chicks that only eat once a day trying to stay skinny," he joked.

"First off, ain't shit skinny over here. Secondly…"

"Oh damn. My bad, my bad," he said laughing.

"Secondly, I eat mostly junk food, and I didn't want to lose my appetite, so I didn't eat anything," she explained.

"Oh, I see," he said as they pulled into the parking lot of The Cheesecake Factory at the Lenox Square Mall.

There was normally a wait on Saturday evenings, but they lucked up and had a table in under fifteen minutes. Once seated, a waitress approached to take their drink orders. They ordered a bottle of Vintage Napa Valley Chardonnay and Thai lettuce wraps for the appetizer. They shared small talk as they looked over their menus, discussing what they were looking for, and what they wanted to accomplish in life.

"Are you guys ready to order?" the waitress asked.

"Of course," Shay answered.

Shay ordered the Chicken Madeira that consisted of sautéed chicken breast topped with fresh asparagus and melted mozzarella cheese, covered with fresh mushroom Madeira sauce, served with mashed potatoes.

Calli ordered the Hibachi Steak that consisted of certified Angus beef hanger steak with shiitake mushrooms, onions, bean sprouts, wasabi mashed potatoes and tempura asparagus.

Shay's meal arrived before Calli's.

"Damn, that looks good," he said.

"Don't be over there drooling over my food. You can't have none," she laughed.

"Damn, I can't get just a piece of the asparagus?" he joked, acting as if he was about to reach across the table.

"Not if you want your hand," Shay said as she waved her fork at him, laughing. His food came a few minutes after hers.

"I've never been here before but I am definitely coming back," Shay said. As they ate.

"I may bring you back one day," he said laughing. They demolished everything on their plates.

"Damn, I don't think I have room for dessert," Calli said, placing his fork down. He was stuffed.

The restaurant was known for giving its patrons huge servings. A couple could order one meal, share it, and be stuffed.

"Well, I do," Shay said waving the waitress over.

"May I have a dessert menu?" she asked.

"Sure, I'll go get one for you," the waitress said then left. She returned with two, handed them each one, and started to clear the table.

"I'll have the caramel pecan turtle cheesecake and a side of vanilla ice cream," Shay said.

"Excellent choice. And you, sir?" the waitress asked.

"I'll have the Adam's peanut butter cup fudge rippled cheesecake with a side of vanilla ice cream as well," Calli said, then closed the menu and handed it back to the waitress.

"Perfect," she said and left their table.

After dinner, the pair left the restaurant hand in hand.

"I really enjoyed myself tonight," Shay said as they cruised down the expressway.

It was a bit cool out, but the night air felt good blowing through her hair, so she let her window down. She was really feeling Calli. She knew that being with him was just a means to an end, but she couldn't deny her feelings.

He was a real gentleman. Back home, she felt like she was stuck with savages. Calli was well-educated, and had multiple things going for himself, if he ever wished to retire from the streets and go legit. She liked the gangsta and gentleman in Calli.

"Likewise," he smiled.

He was feeling Shay as well. He had never opened up to the idea of a relationship or dating, for that matter, because he had seen the dirtiest of chicks. But he could tell Shay was a rare breed and indeed a keeper.

He pulled up to her home twenty minutes later and walked her to her door. He hated the night ended so soon, but he didn't want to pressure her. He wanted to let things flow as they were. When they reached her doorstep, she turned toward him and gazed into his eyes before staring at his kissable lips.

"Thanks for an amazing evening. I haven't been out in quite some time. It was nice," she said.

"I'm glad you enjoyed yourself, ma. We can do this again one day soon. But next, time I'll have to show you my kitchen skills," he said and smiled.

He gazed into her eyes and got lost in them.

Without warning, Shay kissed his lips. She couldn't help herself. They engaged in a passionate kiss.

"Goodnight," she said as she broke the kiss and opened her door.

"Goodnight," he said, then walked back to his car.

Be careful with this one, she thought as she went to shower.

Chapter Eighteen

Monica woke up to find Blue sleeping peacefully next to her. She looked over at the clock on the nightstand and saw that it was a little after 11 am. She never slept that late.

The morning light shining in gave way to view of a huge room. Monica was in awe of the décor. The bedroom was very spacious. She could see that there was a full bar as well as a sitting area in the room. She also could see the Atlanta skyline through the balcony curtains.

Damn, she thought.

She rose and went into the bathroom to the right of the room. The bathroom was the size of the living room in most average apartments. There was a teal and brown color scheme. The toilet was behind another door, sectioned off to itself, as well as the tub and shower. The floors and countertops were marble. There was an area stocked with every kind of bath scrub, beads, shower gel, sponges, and the whole nine.

At first glance, it looked as though a woman decorated the entire bathroom. Hell, it looked like a woman's bathroom. The walk-in shower was huge. About five people could shower at a time and not touch. Monica grabbed some Dove body wash and a sponge and stepped into the shower. She fell in love with the showerhead. She adjusted it and enjoyed the feel of the warm water cascading down her skin. Just as she began to lather up, she heard the door to the shower open.

She looked up to see Blue standing there naked, watching her. She was caught off-guard but quickly recovered. He made her nervous, but she didn't show it. She watched him as he stepped in. She stepped aside and diverted her gaze back to the sponge. She acted as if he wasn't there as she continued to lather her body.

Monica glanced over to see him standing under a showerhead. He had his eyes closed with his hands pressed up against the wall. She admired his muscled body. She was still in awe at how perfect he looked. Monica looked away just as he stepped back and grabbed his towel.

She stepped under the water and began to rinse her body. She felt Blue's hands as he traced his finger down the crack of her ass. Chill bumps rose on her skin. He roughly pinched one of her hardened nipples and pulled her back to him. He turned her around to face him. He looked at her for a few seconds before he leaned down.

Monica puckered her lips, assuming he was about to kiss her, but instead, he put his face in the crease of her neck and bit her as he lifted her off the floor. She wrapped her legs around his waist just as he entered her. He sat her on one of the shower rails and pounded her.

"Ahh," he grunted as he thrusted deeply.

"Oh shit," she moaned, scooting her body to the edge of the rail allowing him to enter as deeply as he could.

"Ummmm," she moaned out.

"Fuck," he moaned out as they both came.

"Nobody can touch you," he said, still inside her. "If I see you in any nigga face, I won't hesitate to stomp a mud hole in your ass," he said menacingly. "Understand?" he asked.

Monica guessed she took too long to answer, because before she knew anything, he had her pushed back in the shower with her back in the corner and her neck pressed against the water pipe.

Blue pushed her hard up against the wall, holding her there, causing the edge of the pipe to cut through her skin. The damage was minimal, but Monica knew that could change if he pushed a little harder.

"Yes," she mumbled. He didn't like how long it took her to answer him. So, he pressed harder causing the pipe to cut more deeply. Blood trickled down her neck.

"Y-y-yes," she said.

"Get out and get dressed. Your clothes are on the bed," he said as he finished his shower and stepped out.

Monica came out shortly after him. She examined the wound on her neck and then went to see what he'd sat out for her.

She found a red deep V-neck, pencil bodysuit. It had a black fishnet design going up the entire side. The bodysuit exposed her breasts, only covering her nipples. There was also a pair of six-inch stiletto pumps. She lifted the bodysuit to see a matching thong set underneath.

The bodysuit fit as if it was glued on. After getting dressed, Blue walked into the room. He looked lip smacking good in his blue Armani suit. His hair was brushed back into a neat ponytail.

"Let's go," he said.

Monica knew she was hated as she walked into the foyer behind Blue and his henchmen. She could feel every eye in the house on her. She could see the hate in each woman's eyes, and lust in the men's eyes.

The only person who looked at her and smiled was Jaz. She had this 'you go, girl, make these hoes hate' expression on her face. She nodded her head at Jaz, who returned the gesture, and they headed out the door.

Three Mercedes Maybach Pullmans drove up. Blue led her to one of the cars and his henchman got into the other two. The two sat back in silence as the car sailed down the expressway.

They pulled up to a huge mansion. There were three other cars parked out front with bodyguards standing in front of each. They were met by a Hispanic guy in a suit.

"Good afternoon," he said.

He led them through the house and out to the patio area where four other men were seated at a long table. There were six bodyguards standing around the table. There were also women of every nationality lingering around the table. She noticed that some were working and others were simply eye candy.

The guys all stood and shook hands. Monica stared at the other men. They were all sexy as hell. She had her eyes on one of the men that came with Blue. She heard Blue call him Quan.

Whap! Whap!

Monica's head flew to the side so fast that her neck snapped.

"Put this bitch in the car," Blue said.

Monica was snatched up by one of Blue's henchmen and hauled off. She was still trying to wrap her brain around what the hell had just happened. Her nose was bleeding and felt like it was broken. She could feel the left side of her face was beginning to swell. She sat in the car for a little over an hour before she saw the door swing open and Blue entered. He didn't say anything to her as they left.

When they pulled back up to the house, he hurriedly snatched her out of the car by her hair and dragged her through the door. Monica tried to free her hair from his grasp, but couldn't. She could feel her hair being ripped from her scalp.

As he dragged her through the foyer and back to his room, Monica could see a few of the girls with a satisfied smirk on their faces. She then felt another punch connect with her jaw and then another one until everything went black.

When she woke up, she glanced around trying to figure out where she was. She realized she was still in Blue's room. She noticed that she couldn't move and saw that she was tied to a pole.

Whap!

Another punch connected with her nose. She felt it break this time.

"Bitch, didn't I just warn you not to fuck with me?" he asked as he delivered another punch.

"W-w-what? What d-did I d-d-do?" she stammered.

He didn't answer her as he grabbed what looked to be a thick black rope. He wrapped the rope around his hand once and swung, connecting with her rib cage. Monica screamed.

She had no way to protect herself from the vicious blows, because both her hands and feet were tied together.

Whack! Whack! Whack!

He swung with all his might, each time opening the skin wherever then rope landed. After so many licks and so much pain, she was unable to scream anymore. She passed out during the beating.

Chapter Nineteen

Monica was still tied up when she woke up. She looked at the clock and saw that she had slept well into the evening. It was a little after ten. She looked around to see if she could spot Blue. He was gone. The only light in the room came from the lap on the nightstand.

Monica was sore and hungry. She also had to use the bathroom. Just as she wondered how long Blue would be gone, he entered the room.

She spoke, "I need to use the bathroom."

He ignored her, pulling things out of his drawers.

"P-please," she mumbled.

He looked over at her, but still ignored her.

"Please, let me use the bathroom," she said again pleading with him.

"You, disrespectful bitch. I couldn't give two fucks if you pissed and shitted on yourself," he said.

"What did I do?" she asked

"Bitch, if I ever see you stare at another nigga, I will gut you like a fucking fish. You wanted to fuck the nigga or some? If that's the case, hoe, I can put you to work in the club. I'm sure you can bring in a few thousand a night, how your pussy can grip a dick," he said.

It took her a few seconds to finally see what she had done. She didn't realize she was looking at Quan so hard. The nigga was so fucking fine, she couldn't help it. She hoped she hadn't fucked up.

For her disrespect, he could make her stay home when it was time to meet with the rest of his crew, making her assignment pointless. She knew she had to fix this now.

"Looking at who? I looked at everyone. I don't know what you're talking about. I would never pull no disrespectful shit like that. Them niggas ain't even my type," she said convincingly.

"Bitch, you gone sit right there until you learn," he said.

He felt insulted, disrespected. The nerve of this bitch. The average bitch would've been hung. He was going to show her as who the fuck he was. He was going to show her that he wasn't to be fucked with.

He left the room and locked the door. It sounded like he put a padlock on the door as well.

"What the fuck?" she said.

She tried to hold her urine for as long as she could, but a few hours later, she could no longer hold it and pissed all over herself. She was beyond disgusted.

***

On the other side of town, Takela and Kayla were staking out one of Blue's trap spots in the Bedford Pine Apartments.

The cool air had the crowd down to a minimum. There were mostly just fiends lingering around. They were sitting in an old Honda

Civic a few houses down, watching. At first glance, the car looked empty.

There were only five guys in the house. They watched as a few other dudes came, but they left after about an hour. They were waiting for their cue.

Since they knew the guys were just a bunch of young dummies, they chose to take the simple route and put two bitches on them. Kayla paid two strippers to go in and distract the guys. She gave them a bullshit story about surprising the men for their hard work. When they saw the wad of money she pulled out, they were in.

"There they are," Kayla said as she watched the two ladies walk up to the door.

A few moments later, they were in. Kayla discreetly put a listening device in a burner phone she'd given the girls.

"Aite, let's get to it," Takela said after noticing the girls had been in the house for about thirty minutes.

The units next door to the apartment were empty on both sides, with a few nodding fiends in them. After hearing the girls on the devices, and using the infrared sensor, they were ready to make their move.

They crept up to the back door. There was never a lock that Kayla couldn't pick. She picked the lock in a matter of seconds, and they were in.

The sensors showed each man in the back of the apartment. The two strippers were giving each man head.

"These niggas dumb as fuck. Is he recruiting from the short bus or what?" Takela asked as she saw the table full up dope and money.

She knew there was over one hundred thousand on the table and at least double that in dope.

They decided to take the dope and money first, since it was in plain view, and the guys were too busy getting their dicks wet to stop them.

Kayla took all the work to the car as Takela stayed as the lookout.

As Kayla came in from the last trip to the car, she heard the back room door open. Takela looked at the sensor to see two men coming their way. They hid behind the sofa. They could see the kitchen and front door from that angle.

"What the fuck?" one of the men asked.

"Where is the shit?" he yelled.

"Trae! Money! James! Get the fuck in here *now*, and bring them bitches!" he yelled. The other guys stormed into the kitchen.

"Brandon, what the fuck you yelling for, nigga? You trying to wake the dead or what?" James asked.

"You see this shit?" he asked.

"Yo, Zach, is this some kind of joke?' Money barked.

"The shit sho ain't funny," James said.

"Why the fuck would I play about some shit like this? Nigga, do I look like I'm playing?" Zach said.

He then looked at the strippers and smacked one.

"What the fuck is going on and who the fuck sent you bitches?" he asked. His voice laced with malice.

"I didn't have shit to do with this," one of the strippers said.

Zach smacked the other one.

"One of you bitches better start talking now, or they gone need dental records to identify you hoes," he said getting angrier by the second.

"Look, I told you, we ain't have shit to do with this. We were just paid to surprise you niggas for the work y'all been putting in."

"Who hired you?" James asked.

"Your boss, obviously," one of the women said.

Whap!

Zach smacked the chick so hard she dropped. He lifted his gun to her head and shot her.

"AHHHHH! What the fuck? We didn't have shit to do with this. I have a son. Please," the other woman begged.

"What's the name of the nigga that sent you?" Zach asked.

"A woman sent me. Please don't kill me. I won't say shit, I swear," she begged.

"Stop lying, hoe. Where the fuck is the money?" Zach said.

"Look, you can take us to the money or you can die right here, right now. It's your decision," James said walking toward her.

"Please, I didn't have shit to do with this. Please, I got a son that needs me. The only reason I'm doing this is to put food on the table. Please, don't kill me," she cried.

Whack!

"Bitch, kill all that fucking noise! Where the fuck is our shit?" Zach yelled becoming impatient.

He knew that Blue would blame him. He wouldn't last a week after this bullshit.

Pop! Pop!

Zach hit the floor with a hole the size of a dime in his head and neck.

"The fuck!" James yelled just before a bullet hit him between the eyes.

Trae and Money pulled out their guns, glancing around to see who'd done the shooting and where it was coming from. Money grabbed the stripper and used her as a shield right before he saw Trae's brains splatter all over the table.

"I'm gone kill this bitch!" he yelled.

"Do what you gotta do?" he heard a female voice say.

That's a bitch, he thought.

"Show your face, or this bitch is gone!" he yelled.

"That bitch a goner regardless, my nigga. The only good witness is a dead one," he heard a female say, then laugh.

The stripper tried to make a run for it.

POW!

A huge hole opened in Money's chest. Kayla walked from behind where Money was standing. The shot caused the stripper to stop. She stood in shock as she watched, and pissed herself.

"Oh, my God. Oh, my God," she cried.

"You don't have to cry for God to save you now, honey. He already has. Say hello for me," Kayla said as she let a shot off, blowing the top of the stripper's head off.

"Aye, what the fuck is going on?" Takela heard a guy ask from outside.

"You go around back," Blue said to two of his henchmen.

Takela and Kayla knew they had to get the fuck out of there. The back door was kicked in, and shots rang out. Kayla and Takela stood in the hallway, blocked by a bookcase. The front door was kicked in next, and the men let more shots off.

Kayla had a clear shot of the men at the back door. She aimed her Glock and fired twice, dropping both of them. Takela picked up one of the machine guns on top of the bookcase and started firing at the front door.

"Ah fuck," she heard one of the men say.

Kayla eased toward the stairs as Takela covered her. The stairs were on the other side of the house and couldn't be seen from the front entrance.

She pulled out her blade kit and discreetly lifted the window. The men were too busy shooting to pay attention to the upstairs windows.

She could clearly see five other men. She placed her gun on the floor and grabbed two blades. She threw them, catching two men in the throat. Before they knew what hit them, they dropped. The other men quickly looked around as one went to see what happened to the fallen men.

"Shit," one said when he saw the blades in their throats.

When he looked up toward the window, a blade pierced his right eye and a bullet pierced his throat. The remaining three men aimed for the upstairs window. The distraction left them open to Takela's bullets as she aimed and hit each man in the head.

Kayla ran back down the stairs to get Takela and leave.

"Check this shit," Quan said as he approached. Each man had their guns drawn.

Takela and Kayla ran up the steps and opened the attic. They climbed in and made their way down to the end of the apartment unit. When they made it to the last unit in the building, they heard a TV playing.

"Them niggas getting robbed," they heard someone say.

"Stop being so damn nosy. Curiosity kills the cat," they heard a lady say.

"Trick please, you are just as nosy. I'm about to go see what's going on now," the woman said.

"Bitch, did you hear all that damn shooting. Your nosy ass will walk straight into a damn bullet."

"Girl, the shooting has stopped and Blue is here. It's a wrap, honey. Now, walk with me."

"Hell nah, I'm straight."

"Bitch, please. I'll buy you a blunt if you do."

"Give me the money now."

"Here you go, hoe, damn. Now come on."

Takela waited a few minutes after she heard the front door close to exit the attic. They left out the back door.

Most of the tenants were on the front surrounding the scene, allowing Takela and Kayla to get to the Honda unnoticed. The street light was blown out over the Honda, giving them the cover they needed. They couldn't pull off just yet. The crowd started to disperse as the police came, so did Blue. Thirty minutes after Blue left, Takela pulled off.

"That's one down," Takela said as she high-fived Kayla.

Chapter Twenty

A full day passed, and Monica had not seen Blue.

She was hungry, dehydrated, and in desperate need of a bath. She had released her bowels all over herself. The room smelled as if there were corpses rotting away in it. No one had come to check on her, not even Jaz.

She knew that Blue had her locked in the room. No one could get in even if they wanted to. She could hear the faint sounds of the other housemates, but it sounded like they were too far away. She didn't bother screaming for help because she knew no one would come to her rescue. She was in and out of consciousness and hallucinating. At times, she saw Blue standing in front of her and her girls. She even saw Jaz standing there with the other girls in the house.

"Yeah, bitch, you ain't so tough now."

"Smile now, hoe."

"Well, look at what we have here. It only took you two hours to get fucked up. A damn shame."

"What's up bottom bitch? I see you really loving it honey," she would hear them laugh at her.

"I got your ass, nigga. Just wait. You gone die by my hands. That's a promise," she said, pointing in the air. "Hahahaha, yeah that ass is mine."

At night, she would cry.

"Blue, baby, why did you leave me? Takela, please help me. Where are you?"

She was slowly breaking.

***

What the fuck is he doing to her? Jaz asked herself.

It had been two whole days since Blue dragged Monica in the house. She couldn't understand what Monica could've done in that small timeframe that had him do her like that.

Blue was known to do some dirty unthinkable shit. She just hoped he hadn't killed her. She could smell a foul scent coming from the room when she was on the third floor.

"Lord please, don't let him kill her," she prayed.

She was getting dressed to go to the club. She had on a slingshot hot pink thong and bra set with matching hot pink pumps. She threw on her coat and headed out. When she made it to the club, she went straight for the bar.

"What's up, Candy?" Jaz said

"Same ole shit, just a different pile. What's up, girl?" Candy responded.

"You already know the drill. Let me get a martini," Jaz said.

"Girl, it looks like you gone need something way stronger than that," she said.

"Surprise me," Jaz said as she lifted her hand.

Candy mixed her a drink and gave the gold liquid to her.

"This will hit the spot," Candy said.

Jaz went into her pocket and pulled out two pills. She called them her pimp. After taking them, she would do whatever it was they wanted her to do. She took them both and drank her drink.

"Damn," she said, "Give me another one."

Candy obliged.

Jaz drank two more drinks then started to make her rounds. She noticed the same stud that was there earlier last week. She walked toward her table.

"Lap dance," Jaz said.

Takela nodded.

Jaz led her to a private area for the dance.

"Monica needs your help. You have to get her the fuck out of there," Jaz said.

She smiled while she danced, trying to act normal.

Takela went along with it.

"What did she do? What's happening to her?" she asked.

"He has her looked in the room. She left with him a few days ago. They weren't gone long, but when he came back, he came in dragging and beating her. She has been in the room ever since. He hasn't been back and I think she hurt. There is this real foul odor coming from his room. It's getting stronger and stronger," Jaz explained still dancing.

From the normal eye, it looked like Jaz was giving a hell of a lap dance and flirting.

Takela was throwing bills on her as they spoke.

"Is there a way you can get me in there?" Takela asked.

"What do you mean get you in there?" Jaz asked.

"You just said I need to come get her. Can you get me in there?"

"He will kill you before you make it to her. I've seen how he looks at her. He isn't just going to let her go. You gone have to bring all you have to this, and more, or you're fucked," Jaz said as her first song ended.

She knew Takela would have to start throwing some more bills or she would have to walk away because she knew Jeff was watching the camera. To her relief, Takela pulled out another wad of money.

"Let me worry about that. Monica is doing what she is getting paid to do, just go with it. We got it. Blue will no longer be, in a matter of time."

"Huh? Stop talking in codes. Shit, if you don't trust me, then you've already fucked up," Jaz said.

"Not really. If I didn't trust you, you wouldn't have made it out of this club last week, and if I feel any sign of treason, you won't

116

make it out tonight. If Blue was all we wanted, we could've been had him," Takela said.

"I want in," Jaz said.

Takela just looked at her.

"That nigga killed my whole fucking family and sold my little sister, all because my mom told my dad there was something about him she didn't trust. She just fucked up and spoke those words in front of the wrong motherfucker," Jaz said. "I promised my sister I would come for her, and just when she was leaving with that fat fucking pedophile, she grabbed Quan's gun and shot herself. She was only thirteen," Jaz said. She was getting too emotional.

Takela smacked her on her ass and said, "One more dance sexy," in her ear.

When Jaz leaned her head forward Takela said, "Keep your shit together. You're drawing unwanted attention. I will let you handle yours when the time is right. Monica can handle her own. She won't be there much longer. When I come for her, be ready."

Jaz looked down to see that Takela had put a stack in the waist band of her thong.

Chapter Twenty-One

Blue walked through the door furious. He couldn't believe a motherfucker had the nerve to rob him.

The instant he walked in his room, he was hit with a foul odor that caused him to gag. He looked over to see Monica unconscious.

"Fuck, I forgot all about this bitch," he said.

He could see that she was fucked up. Exactly how he wanted her to be. He went to the bar got one of the buckets he used for ice and filled it with cold water. He poured the water in Monica's face. She woke up choking, then she tried to catch some of the water with both hands and began to drink. This caused her to choke more.

Blue didn't like seeing her like that, but he had to do what was necessary to break her down. He didn't want to get rid of her, but he knew he had to break her in order to control her. He beat the hell out of some of the weaker women to control them, and he drugged the strong-willed ones. This kept them in line and coming back. He simply shot the ones he couldn't control or didn't have the patience to deal with or break.

Monica would've been one of the ones he killed, but he couldn't bring himself to do it. She challenged him. Women didn't seem to understand that no matter the man, they always liked a challenge. They lived for a challenge.

A man could be abusive as hell, beat the hell out of every woman he got, and they'd take it, rarely fighting back and showing fear. Then, he'd meet this one chick that ain't going for that shit, and would go round after round with his ass; would even go as far as to cut that nigga, and all and he was gone love the shit out of that bitch. That'd be the one he'd be crazy as hell about and couldn't live without.

Where he didn't love, or just showed no love for, the chicks before her, the world was gone know he loved that bitch. He could no longer take the smell as he called out for Jaz.

"Get her in the bathroom and clean her up," he ordered.

"I'll have someone come clean that shit up," he said and left the room.

"What the fuck? Monica! Monica!" Jaz yelled.

Monica's eyes were rolling, and she couldn't keep her head up. She was so weak. Jaz ran to the tub and filled it with warm water. She added some of the Dove body wash to help with the scent.

She undressed Monica, holding her breath the entire time, then carried her to the bath. Monica slowly became alert and started to look around.

"Oh my God," Jaz said as she saw some of the bruises Blue had left. He was careful not to bruise her arms or any other visible body parts. He'd bruised her ribs, back, and upper thighs. Once she put on clothes, they couldn't be seen.

119

Jaz bathed Monica, then she let the water out. She ran her more water, this time with Epsom salt and bilberry extracts, to make the marks vanish and to increase the level of vitamin c. She laid Monica back and let her soak. She went downstairs to find something for her to eat. As she passed, she saw a cleaning crew, cleaning up the mess. She returned to Monica with a chicken salad, crackers, and a bottle of water.

The cleaning crew was gone, and the room looked as good as new. It even smelled fresh. Monica was still soaking in the tub. Jaz shut the door and began to feed her.

"Are you feeling a little better?" she asked.

"Yes," Monica replied.

"What happened? Why did he do this to you?" Jaz asked.

Monica laid her had back and closed her eyes as if she was trying to remember.

"We went to a meeting and I looked a one of the men there. I guess I looked a second too long, because he became furious and here I am now," she said, not really wanting to relive the ordeal.

"Damn, this is fucked up. Do you know a girl name Tee?" Jaz asked.

"Who?" Monica said.

"Tee. She came into the strip club. She asked about you. At first, I didn't really say anything, but she came back yesterday and I told her where you were and what was happening. I didn't know if the nigga killed you or what. I told her she needed to come help you."

"Yes, I know her," she said.

She stopped there because she didn't feel right talking to Jaz. She looked at the door and then back at Jaz. Jaz got up and closed the room door after assuring they were alone, then she closed the bathroom door.

Monica proceeded, "I'm here to do a job. We have a contract to kill Blue."

"Well, why the nigga ain't dead yet? You been here long enough with plenty of opportunities to do so," Jaz said getting upset.

"The contract is not just for Blue. Trust me, if it was just him, he would be dead by now. If we just get Blue, they will just find someone else to replace him. We have a contract on all the bosses. The entire organization."

"And how in the fuck do you plan to kill the entire organization? That's like trying to assassinate the Pope. You will never get close enough. They're too careful for shit like this."

"Well, the nigga ain't the Pope, and neither is the organization. Why the fuck you think I'm on the inside? It'll be easier to do. I've already accomplished my first goal. It won't be hard."

"It will be if you can't communicate with your girl. How in the hell were y'all supposed to communicate?" Jaz asked

"That wasn't my job. It was hers and as you can see, she did it well," Monica said.

"So, what now? Find the meeting place and set it ablaze," Jaz said sarcastically.

"Exactly," Monica said nonchalantly. She was still a bit weak, so Jaz had to help her out the tub and into her clothes.

"I'm here to help you with whatever you need, just let me know. I want that nigga dead," Jaz said.

"Acting off emotions can be dangerous and can get us both killed. Put your feelings in your back pocket on this one," Monica said. Jaz looked up in time to see someone peeking in the room. When she ran to the door and looked out, no one was there.

"Fuck," she said under her breath.

When she made it back to Monica's side, she was out.

Chapter Twenty-Two

Over the next few weeks, Takela and Kayla hit more of Blue's spots, crippling his men. They needed to take out as many of his crewmembers as possible. They were expendable and Blue's frontline defense.

Crippling his frontline would make it easier to touch him and the others at the meeting without a major gun fight. But there would, indeed, be a gun fight.

They really had no use for the drugs they had stolen, or the well over four million dollars.

Blue was furious.

Quan's pillow talk would be the death of him. He told Kayla exactly what they planned to do when they would do it, and how. He told her how Blue suspected someone close to home and all. They learned most of what they knew from Quan and Jaz.

Shay hadn't really been bringing much information to the table. She said she had been taking things slow because Calli was no fool, and she was right to do so.

Takela and Kayla didn't tell Shay what they'd been up to. They were going to split the money equally, but they didn't want to hear her mouth lecturing them about how they could be putting Monica in danger.

If the bitch was so concerned, she should've volunteered, Takela thought.

Blue was out in the streets trying to figure out what the hell was going on, and who had crossed him. He felt it was an inside job, because he knew nobody else was stupid enough, nor know enough. Shit was crazy in the streets.

Blue, not paying attention to home, allowed Monica and Jaz the space and opportunity they needed to devise a plan to escape without notice.

They watched the men in the house around the clock and learned their schedules. With Blue not being there, security became too comfortable. They began to slack and help themselves to the women. Most nights, instead of doing their jobs securing the house, they were laid up.

Monica found out that the meeting was going to be the following Friday night. It was Wednesday. Their plan to leave would take place Thursday night. They didn't want to leave too early before the meeting. Thursday night would be perfect. Even if Blue suspected something, it would be too late to reschedule the meeting, because everyone would already be en route.

Blue wouldn't be home on Thursday night, making the odds of not getting caught better. Kayla informed them that Blue would be hitting a crew he had working on the Southside of Atlanta that night, collection night.

He got word that the niggas had loose lips and were pocketing his money. When he sent his men to collect, they were short a few thousand. The last few collections were short, and Blue became suspicious. He was suspecting any nigga that moved wrong, and he was ready to clean house. He was at war with the streets and he wouldn't sleep until he located his money. He refused to keep taking losses.

They found out through Quan the location of the meeting and who would be there. The meeting would be held in a penthouse suite located on the Eastside of Atlanta. They learned the time of the meeting, 8 pm, through Jaz. All they had to do was sit back and wait.

Jaz had an eerie feeling that she couldn't shake. She tried to wave it off as nervousness, but she felt something was wrong. She kept going back to the night she and Monica spoke in Blue's room.

She could've sworn she saw someone peeking in, but when she went to investigate, no one was there. Still, she waved the feeling off.

Chapter Twenty-Three

Ding Dong. Ding Dong.

The sound of the doorbell caught Calli's attention.

He was in the kitchen preparing dinner for himself and Shay.

Outside of the drama of being in the game with Blue, Calli had been kicking it with Shay heavy.

She's wife material no doubt, he thought.

He had taken her out several times, and each time they enjoyed themselves. At first, she had this good girl persona going on when it came to sex with him. But after the fourth date, she found him irresistible and let him make love to her in her home.

He stayed over that entire weekend. By Sunday, neither of them wanted to part, but life called and they had to answer. That was three weeks ago.

"Hello, beautiful," he said.

"Hey there, yourself," she said as she kissed him. "Something smells good."

"I know," he said cockily as he led the way to the kitchen.

She just smiled.

She was feeling Calli just as much as he was feeling her. At first, she was confused at how she could actually fall for someone who could befriend a man like Blue. She saw Blue as the scum of the earth. What else would you call a man who sold women as sex slaves? She couldn't understand how Calli could watch him do this and not interfere. How he could play a part in it all?

It wasn't until she actually got to know Calli that she began to let her guard down. She could see the man he truly was. Calli didn't necessarily agree with what Blue did, but he understood that he was going to do what he wanted to do, whether Calli had problems with it or not. Calli only took part in the drug-related interactions.

He wasn't one to mess up business simply because he disagreed with his boy's way of living. He hated to see Blue do what he did to women, which was why he stayed away from Blue's crib.

They had been boys for years. Calli and Blue was brothers from different mothers. He chose not to turn his back on him simply because of his career choice. Besides, Calli had made millions in the game. He just needed someone to help him spend it.

Shay walked toward the dining area where Calli prepared a candle lit dinner. The burning fireplace set the mood. He even had soft music playing in the background. She loved a man who could be a beast in the streets, but knew to put it away when he came home. A man that could still be romantic.

She saw in him what should've been easy to find at home, but every man she ran into was lacking. The men she had been with didn't know the definition of romantic. They called taking you to IHOP, and fucking to one of Future's songs, romantic.

Shay just smiled as she watched him remove a dish from the oven. She loved to see a man do his thing in the kitchen. He fixed their plates, sat them on the table, and then pulled her chair out for her to sit.

"Dinner is served," he said.

"Tonight, we're having linguine all'aragosta o all'astice (linguine with lobster) and bruschetta (antipasto grilled bread) served with Sardinian white wine," he said in his best Italian accent. Then he took his seat.

"This is really good," she said as she dug in.

It took everything in her not to go all in. The food was lip smacking good.

"Who taught you to cook like this?" she asked.

"No one can teach you how to cook, in my opinion. Cooking comes naturally. You just learn how to make dishes," he answered. "I love Italian and Mexican food, so I learned how to make about any dish," he said.

"I can burn a little as well. I'm not on your level yet, but I can get there with practice," she said with a smile.

"You think?"

"No. I know," she said confidently.

"That's what's up. We shall see," he began to clear the table, then they both laid by the fireplace and watched the flames dance.

The soft plush rug felt heavenly against her skin. She enjoyed the feel of his arms around her. She felt secure with him. Shay tried her hardest not to think about the job they were there to do, but it was hard. She knew this would be the last time she would see Calli. She didn't want it to end, but she knew being with Calli was just a temporary job. She knew she had to let him go. If only she hadn't caught feelings, it wouldn't be so hard. He was everything she wanted all wrapped in one.

I finally find what I'm looking for only to have to let him go, she thought.

She tried to clear her head and enjoy their last night together.

"What's on your mind, beautiful?" he asked, turning her toward him and looking into her eyes.

"You," she said as she mounted him and bent to kiss him. They were engrossed in a lustful kiss.

"Make love to me, Calli," she said.

He laid her on her back, removed her clothes, and climbed on top her. He slowly kissed her lips, then her neck. He took one of her nipples in his mouth as he rubbed her other nipple. He switched to her other nipple and sucked it lightly. She moaned.

He kissed his way down to her navel and bikini line. He parted her legs and kissed the insides of her thighs. He gently sucked her thighs.

Shay arched her back as she felt his lips on her clit and he passionately kissed her pussy.

"Ohh," she moaned as he used his tongue to part her lips. He inserted his tongue into her slowly. "Oh my God," she moaned.

"Yess," she cried as she came.

Calli lapped up her juices and began to kiss her thighs again. He made his way down to her perfectly manicured feet and kissed them. She had never had a man suck her toes, but she loved the feel of his tongue on her feet so much that she almost came again when he took her big toe into his mouth.

He gave her other foot the same attention, then worked his way back to her lips. He loved how the fireplace illuminated her skin, giving it a special glow.

He kissed her hungrily. She returned his hunger, devouring him. She loved her taste on his tongue. She helped him remove his clothes and admired his body, a true work of art.

He caressed her ass cheeks and entered her.

She loved the way he felt inside of her. His dick had a curve that made her feel like no other.

He felt her clench as he hit her spot and sped up his strokes. She screamed out his name as she came all over his dick and the rug under her.

She grabbed his face and kissed him as he started to give her long, deep strokes. She drove him crazy biting his bottom lip as he found her g-spot again. He brought them both to a powerful orgasm. He came deep inside her, and they both fell fast asleep.

Shay awoke in the wee hours of the morning. She looked at Calli sleeping so peacefully. She blew him a kiss and said her final goodbye.

Chapter Twenty-Four

"Aye, Jaz," AJ, one of Blue's henchmen, called out.

"What's up?" she responded.

"Blue wants you down at the club tonight. Get ready. The car leaves in an hour."

"But, I've never worked on Thursdays," Jaz said.

"He got some cats coming in from Detroit, and he wants his best on it tonight."

"Um, okay," Jaz said and walked on hastily, in search of Monica.

Her working at the club was definitely going to ruin their plans to leave. The club didn't close until 3am and Blue wouldn't allow any of the women to leave until the last trick left the building. She spotted Monica going into the hall bath.

"We have a serious problem," she said pulling Monica inside and securing the door.

"What's wrong?" Monica asked

"Blue wants me down at the club tonight."

"I thought you didn't work on Thursdays?" Monica said, getting pissed.

"I don't but he has special guests coming and he wants his best on the job. You know them other lazy bitches ain't pulling in nowhere near the amount of money I'm pulling in," Jaz said.

"Okay, we still can follow through with the plan, we'll just have to wait until you get off," Monica said pacing the floor.

She refused to be in Blue's home any longer.

"You sure?" Jaz asked with a look of uncertainty on her face.

"Yeah. We got it. The plan is the same. I'll be waiting on you, right here. Be ready." Monica told Jaz.

Jaz nodded and went to her room to get dressed.

***

Time was going by extremely slow at the club. Jaz had been giving private dances all night, hoping that by the time she was through dancing to a few songs time would've flown past. But, to her dismay, it moved slowly. Especially since she was watching the clock.

An hour before closing, Jaz had already left the dance floor and was preparing to leave. She had made well over the quota Blue set for each woman.

Normally, if Blue was there, he wouldn't let them leave the dance floor until the exact closing time, no matter if they met the quota or not. Jaz's hands began to sweat during the ride home. She was anxious to be free of Blue's grasp. She had special plans for his ass. When the driver let her and some of the other girls out, she hurriedly walked in and found Monica.

"You go ahead, and wait on me at the hill. I need to go pick up something," Jaz said.

"Hell nah, leave it and come on while the coast is clear," Monica ordered.

"No, I have to get it," Jaz said. "I will be right behind you," she said.

With that Monica, left through the side exit of the house. Blue normally had his man Jay at that door, but he was upstairs getting his dick wet. She eased out without notice.

Jaz had been saving money for the day she would leave. She had it hidden in her room in her mattress, a little over $20,000. When she went to retrieve it, she ran into nosy ass Tasha.

What is this lazy hoe still doing up? she wondered.

She bypassed her, only for her to follow Jaz into her room trying to spark a bullshit conversation to be nosy.

"How did it go tonight? Tasha asked.

"Like every other night," Jaz answered bitterly.

"Oh," Tasha said with an attitude.

When Tasha left her room, Jaz grabbed her money and eased back down the steps.

"Jaz," someone called out, startling her. She couldn't see who called her name.

"Jaz," she heard again

"What?" she answered.

"Mya, is that you?" Jaz asked finally, catching the voice.

Mya was one of the girls Blue had snatched up when she was fourteen. He had also snatched her twin Nya. They were now eighteen. She was one of the quiet ones. She'd barely ever said a word since she'd been there.

Blue thought it was out of fear, but it wasn't. Her and her sister were identical. Blue was initially going to sell them both, but he found that he could make more money putting the twins on a pole each night. They had bodies most women dreamed of. To the naked eye, they appeared flawless with their honey brown complexions and long wavy hair.

"Don't do it, Jaz," Mya said.

"Huh?" Jaz said feigning ignorance, "What are you talking about?"

"Those guards aren't stupid. They see everything you do even when you think they don't. I'm sure if I could put two and two together, then so can they," Mya said, not telling her what she really wanted to say.

"I'll be fine, Mya. I will come back for you, but first I have to get out of here. I have something planned when I leave. It'll all be over Saturday. Wait for me and be safe," Jaz said.

She gave Mya a tight hug and proceeded down the stairs, headed toward the side door. The coast was still clear. When she made it out, she saw a light go on toward the steps. She quickly closed the door silently.

"Going somewhere?" Jay asked pointing his Glock in her face.

Jaz was startled as she turned around to see Jay, Jeff, Star, and Marcus all standing with guns aimed at her.

"That bitch ain't that slick," she heard a voice say. Then she saw Tasha, Chell, and Tracy walk out the side door.

"Yeah, you thought you had the perfect getaway, didn't it? Blue gone love me for this one. Did y'all catch that other bitch?" Chell asked.

"Nah, but we will. We got niggas on the lookout," Jay said.

"Have y'all called Blue?" Tasha said.

"Yeah, but he ain't answering," Marcus said.

Jaz felt a sharp pain in the back of her head, and then everything went black.

Chapter Twenty-Five

Monica knew in her gut something was wrong. Takela was waiting for her three blocks over. She refused to leave without Jaz. She'd stayed planted in the same spot for over an hour with no word.

"Monica, she's not coming. We have to go," Takela told her.

"No! We wait!" Monica yelled.

"For how long, Monica? It's been over an hour and still no word. Don't be stupid, Monica, something happened. There is nothing we can do for her now without risking ourselves. We're not prepared to go in there, especially without Kayla or Shay," Takela said.

"She'll be dead by then. Blue will kill her," Monica said low.

If it hadn't been for Jaz, Monica didn't know how she would've carried out her mission. Jaz had saved her. With great sadness, Monica got in the car with Takela, vowing to come back to burn that house to the ground and everyone in it.

That was, after she got Jaz out.

***

When Jaz came to, she realized she was tied to a weight lifting bench. She looked around and realized she was naked and in the exact same spot she'd found Monica.

She heard footsteps approaching and pretended to be unconscious. She felt a hard blow connect with her mouth.

"Wake up, bitch," Blue said.

She opened her eyes to find Blue's cold eyes looking back at her with five other men. She had never seen them before. They were his street soldiers.

"Where the fuck is she?" he asked in a cold tone.

Jaz didn't say a thing, so he hit her again this time connecting with her nose. She couldn't shield herself from his blows because her hands were tied around the bench.

"Where is she?" he said as he punched her after every word.

Jaz still didn't talk.

Blue beat Jaz into a bloodied pulp. During the beating, she never once cried out. She kept her mouth closed as he tried his hardest to beat her to death.

"So, you can't talk now. We'll see how long that last," he said as he pulling off his thick leather belt.

He then beat her with his belt. The first few blows landed on her lower half, but Blue made his way up to her chest, neck, and face. He swung the belt viciously until he became tired.

Jaz was in and out of consciousness, but she still didn't say a word. This frustrated Blue more.

He pulled a small razor from his pocket and started to cut small gashes on her legs, working his way up to her neck. He then pulled out a jar filled with fire ants and dumped them on her before leading his crew back down the stairs.

Blue knew she wasn't going to talk. There was only one option left for her, death.

The ants began to bit her instantly. She couldn't cry or scream if she wanted to. A few minutes after Blue left, Chell and Tasha came up.

"That's what you get you uppity ass get," Chell said.

"Bitch, you chose to walk around here with you head held high like you so much better than the rest of us. In case you haven't noticed, sweetie, we are all in the same predicament. So, don't get it twisted, bitch," Tasha said, right before Jaz lost consciousness again.

She woke up to the sting of Raid as AJ sprayed it to kill the ants. He then threw a bucket of water mixed with peroxide on her. It damn near sent her into shock.

"Kill me," she said. "Just kill me."

"Nah bitch, we not making it that easy," Tasha said.

"Go ahead. Y'all can have this bitch," she said to the three guys that came into the room. They looked like dope fiends. Their clothes were raggedy and Jaz could smell them before they got to her. Tasha, Chell, and AJ watched as the men had their way with her.

An hour later, they all headed back downstairs. Tasha wanted to slit Jaz's throat, but Blue told them he would handle her. He had no idea what'd just happened to Jaz.

"Oh my God! Jaz, wake up. Get up. We're getting you out of here."

Jaz tried to focus on the voice, but she was in and out of consciousness.

"Jaz, it's me, Mya," Mya announced as she began to cut the rope.

"Mya, hurry up before they come back down here," Nya said.

"Jaz, please wake up. Stay alert," Mya said. She picked up one of the ice cubes from the floor and rub it on Jaz's forehead.

"Someone's coming," Nya said. There was no time for them to hide.

"What the fuck?" Chell said.

Before she could run back down the stairs, she was met with a blow to her forehead with a hammer that stopped her in her tracks. Nya beat Tasha's face in with the hammer.

"Nya, that's enough," Mya said. Nya had this crazed look in her eyes.

Finally, she said, "Come on, we have to go *now*."

They ran toward the steps to see if the coast was clear, it was. Just as they were getting ready to help Jaz down the steps, they heard a loud boom.

Chapter Twenty-Six

Blue, Quan, and Calli met in the lobby of the Ritz Carlton two hours before they were scheduled to be there. Blue wanted to scope out the building and have his men in place.

Normally, nothing ever happened at the meetings, but Blue wasn't taking any chances with the way shit had been turning out for him lately. He was sure his t's were crossed and i's were dotted.

"If a nigga act stupid tonight, they will be toe-tagged," he said to Quan.

Most of the bosses arrived an hour early. The rest came right at the scheduled time.

"Let's get down to business," one of the men said.

***

Takela, Monica, Kayla, and Shay were posted a few blocks over waiting for the perfect time to strike.

They counted four security guards, two at the front entrance and two at the back. They had no way of knowing how many people were inside so they knew they had to draw them out.

"Let's get this shit over with," Shay said.

Kayla threw two knives that dropped the men at the front door. Takela took out the men at the back and side doors with her Tippmann X7 sniper rifle. Monica blew the front door open after throwing a C4 bomb through the front window. She was sure the explosion could be heard up to a mile away so they had to move fast.

The explosion caused the men to react slowly allowing the women the upper hand. Takela saw three men running down the steps and began to drop them one by one.

"Monica, where is he keeping Jaz?" Takela asked.

"In the attic," Monica answered.

"I'll go get her. Cover me," she said.

The shock of the explosion faded, and Blue's men were armed and ready. It sounded like World War II was going on. Shots were being fired from every direction.

As Monica made her way to the back staircase leading to the attic, she ran into one of the Chell's lap dogs, Meka.

"Bitch, what do you think you are doing?" she asked.

Monica didn't reply. She just ran up and began to pistol whip her. She didn't stop swinging until Meka stopped moving. She put a bullet in her head and ran up the steps.

"Jaz!" she yelled out. "Jaz!"

"She's right here," Monica heard someone say.

Mya walked around the corner and pointed to Jaz. Monica raised her gun at Mya, ready to fire.

"No," Jaz said. "She helped me leave," Jaz said in a low tone. "She's good people," she said.

Monica saw her sister round the corner.

"Are y'all strapped?" Monica asked.

The shook their heads.

"How the fuck were y'all preparing to leave?" Monica asked sarcastically. She handed each one of them a gun.

"Stay close," she said.

"But, she can't walk on her own," Mya said.

Monica knew that would slow them down. Under normal circumstances, she would've left her. But this wasn't normal.

"Can you hold her up?" Monica asked.

"Yes," she replied.

Monica ran over to the breaker box and turned off the power in the house. Each gun had a heat sensing scope, so she would be able to see everyone coming. She saw two henchmen coming toward the steps and aimed.

"Where you at, Tee? I got her," Monica yelled.

Takela barely heard her over the gunshots.

"Alright, let's move!" she yelled.

"If you want to leave house alive, I suggest you do so now," Kayla said to the women.

They all scattered like roaches.

Shay ran through the house, attaching C4 bombs to each wall she passed. She took out eight of the men in her path. Kayla shot everything moving, man or woman. They all were targets to her. Takela saw Monica as she ran down the stairs with two other women beside her.

"What the fuck are you doing? We didn't come for them, just her," Takela said.

Mya aimed her gun toward Takela and let off two rounds. Takela looked back and saw two men laying on the floor. They had crept behind her and were aiming at her when Mya spotted them.

"Let's go," was all Takela said.

All seven women ran out of the house toward their car. They had to squeeze in to make room.

As they drove off, Monica hit the switch to the C4 bombs and watched as the house exploded. She was satisfied now.

"Next stop, Ritz Carlton," Kayla said.

Chapter Twenty-Seven

"What the fuck did you just say?" Quan asked.

He could barely hear AJ over the gunshots. It sounded like mayhem on the other end.

"We getting hit! Bitches came in here blowing shit up and shooting any nigga that moved," AJ yelled.

"Fuck," Quan said. "We can't have this shit now."

"We tried to call Blue, but that nigga ain't answering. Shit is all the way fucked up over here. They dropping us like flies, man. Send some help, man," AJ said.

Quan heard a loud explosion, then the call disconnected. He walked back inside the suite and signaled for Blue and Calli to step out.

"Some shit going down at the house. AJ claim some bitches just ran in."

"Bitches?" Blue said, cutting him off.

"Yes, bitches just ran in there blowing up shit. He said they hit him hard and they dropping like flies. He said he was trying to call you, but of course, you didn't answer. Then I heard a loud ass explosion, and the call disconnected," Quan explained.

"What the fuck?" Calli said.

"Yeah man, shit is crazy," Quan said.

Blue just stood there with the crazed look in his eyes. He couldn't believe someone had run in his crib, bitches at that.

He couldn't afford this type of negativity now, not with this meeting going down. He would appear weak. They would instantly snatch the throne from under him if they got wind of what had just happened. He wanted to go on a killing spree, but he knew now wasn't the time. He had to get through the meeting first.

Everything was going well so far, and he didn't want to fuck anything up.

"Look, go back in there like this shit ain't happening. We can't lose this connect. Trouble in-house is never a good look. We'll deal with this shit when the meeting is over," he said.

They walked back in and continued as if nothing happened.

***

"What's your name?" Takela asked

"Mya, and this is my sister, Nya," she answered.

"I'm Takela, Kayla, and Shay," Takela said pointing to each woman.

"So, how is your shooting?"

"Okay, I guess. I'm no professional, but I hit my target. Our dad taught us to shoot" Mya said.

She looked in back to see Monica cradling Jaz's head.

Jaz was in really bad shape, but she was conscious. She knew they needed to get her to a doctor. They decided to take Jaz to Shay's house to lie down. She was no good to them in her current state and would only slow them down. They dropped her off and then regrouped, putting on bulletproof vests and loading up.

"These are my babies. Treat them right," Takela said, handing Mya and Nya both of her Ruger 9mm pistols.

She gave them two extra clips and provided both of them with two Kyoketshu-Shogei knives a piece. Takela grabbed her 9mm Berta and her blades. She put her small twenty-two in her ankle holster.

Kayla grabbed her twelve-piece stainless steel S-Force Kunai knife case, and both of her Desert Eagle .44 Magnum guns and holster.

Shay had two Glock 17s in her waist holster, and she armed herself with a few grenades and knives.

Monica armed herself with her SIG Sauer P226 guns and a few homemade bombs. She grabbed a ceramic container that she put battery acid in. She also grabbed a few knives, too. She, like her girls, all knew that at the end of the day, there would never be enough bullets.

Armed and ready, they headed out in three different bulletproof Chevy Tahoe's. The women split into three groups of three; Takela and Kayla, Mya and Monica, and Nya and Shay. They drove right behind each other.

"So, what's the plan?" Kayla said laughing already knowing the plan. She lived for this shit.

"Kill them all. Leave no one standing," Takela said.

Chapter Twenty-Eight

"This concludes this meeting," one of the bosses said.

The men stood and shook hands. They all headed to the parking garage across the street from the Ritz. As the men got in their vehicles, preparing to leave, there was a loud explosion.

The first two trucks parked to the right of the exit exploded. There was a second explosion on the left side of the garage, sending three cars up in flames.

"What the fuck!?" Blue screamed as he struggled to gain his balance.

He couldn't believe the scene unfolding in front of him. He watched as the men ran to their cars to take cover. It was complete mayhem.

He ran toward the nearest truck to him. It was one of his henchmen's cars. He pulled out his gun and began firing alongside his man.

"What the fuck is this? You set us up!" one of the Hispanic bosses said.

"No. No, I don't know what the fuck is going on," Blue yelled, but the man wasn't trying to hear him out.

The man pointed his gun at Blue, but before he could pull the trigger, Calli blew the man's brains out. Calli ran to Blue's side, handed him an additional clip, and started firing.

Blue took notice of the black Tahoe parked a few feet away. He fired on it, but his bullets had no effect on the car.

He saw the passenger window roll down and someone shooting out of the window. He aimed at the opened window and fired until his clip was empty.

"Calli," Blue called out, signaling for Calli to shoot toward the car while he reloaded. Blue knew he hit his target, because he heard a woman yell out.

"Argh!" Nya yelled out.

Shay looked over to see Nya was hit in the arm.

Fucking amateur! Shay thought. *Why the fuck would this stupid bitch have the window halfway down, exposing her damn self?*

Just as Shay reached over to let the window up, a bullet pierced Nya's throat.

Shay looked out to see Calli aiming at her. She could tell he couldn't see her clearly. She hurriedly let the window up and put the truck in reverse.

"Fuck!" Shay yelled as she watched the life slip from Nya.

Monica hit the trigger in her hand causing more cars to go up in flames, exposing her targets hiding behind them.

She was looking for Blue, but she couldn't find him in the chaos.

148

Where the fuck is he? she thought.

Mya was in the passenger seat shooting everything that moved. She didn't miss her target. She was on a mission. Like Monica, Mya was looking for Blue. She secretly hoped she found him before Monica did.

They both spotted Blue at the same time.

"There he is!" Monica yelled.

She saw that Blue had three guys standing beside him shooting. Monica aimed for the man by the passemger door and Mya aimed for the man at the driver's side door, crouched down, shooting toward Takela and Kayla. She fired, blowing his brains in Blue's face.

The last guy standing by Blue ducked and went toward the back of the truck, out of their line of fire. Blue remained in the same spot, firing toward Monica's truck.

Mya jumped out the truck and went for him.

"No!" Monica yelled after her.

She jumped out the car behind her and covered her.

A few of the men saw her jump out and aimed for her. Monica took each one out with expert precision.

Each man that ran toward her was cut down with Monica's blades. She caught the first guy in the side of his throat twisted the blade and stuck the other blade in the opposite side of his throat doing the same, decapitating him. She was vicious with her blades cutting down eleven men in under three minutes.

Takela and Kayla were just as vicious. They took out seven of the bosses and their entourages. They knew they would be taking out entire teams, but this was more like taking out an entire army.

Takela and Kayla alone had well over thirty bodies under their belt in a matter of minutes. It seemed as though the men just kept coming, but with Monica, Mya, Takela, and Kayla working together, they dropped almost every man standing. There were only three other men shooting.

"Where the fuck is Shay and Nya?" Takela asked, noticing the third Tahoe MIA.

She knew one of them had to be hurt, but alive, considering they managed to drive away.

Shay sped out of the parking lot. They had major fire coming their way, and she needed Nya as her back up, but since Nya was now dead, she had to vacate. She knew her girls had it covered. She drove frantically to her home.

Blue was in a state of panic once he noticed that just about every man was down. He could see Quan still busting shots.

Takela fired hitting Quan in the throat. The next shot hit him in the center of his forehead.

Blue was in a state of panic once he noticed that just about every man was down.

All of his men had been killed expect for Calli. The bosses had turned on them, but they had all been killed as well. There was no movement in the garage.

"Come on, we need to get the fuck out of here and regroup," Blue heard Calli whisper.

They heard the faint sounds of sirens in the distance. They crouched down and went toward the side door. Calli open the door and crawled out unnoticed.

"Blue," Mya called out.

Blue recognized the voice and turned in the direction of the voice.

"Bitch, I'm going to kill you!" he fumed.

He couldn't believe she was bold enough to pull this shit. He couldn't believe the bitch managed to get away. She was the weakest link in his eyes. She never fought back, even when she watched him kill her entire family. He didn't even have her tied up, but she didn't try to run. She grabbed her twin, balled up in a corner, and cried.

She aimed and shot Blue in the knee. Calli didn't realize Blue wasn't behind him until he made it to the corner. Once he exited the side door, he ran across the street.

"Damn nigga, we need to get some wheels, and fast," he said.

"Blue," he called out, looking back.

"Fuck!" he said when he noticed Blue wasn't with him. He didn't want to leave him. He was out of bullets and a sitting duck out there.

He heard the gun shot and saw a silhouette of a man fall through the window. It was no use going back, because he knew it was Blue. With the law getting close, he knew he had to go. Shay's house was the closest to his location, so he headed there.

Chapter Twenty-Nine

"Bitch, you better kill me," Blue said with malice. He was fuming mad that he had been setup by this bitch.

"So this," Blue waved his hand around, "is all you?" he asked.

"Nope," Mya said.

"Figures. Bitch, you ain't nowhere near bright enough," he said laughing.

Mya stuck her knife through his right cheek all the way through to his left cheek and pulled it out.

"Argh!" he yelled out in agony.

Monica walked up behind her. Blue was speechless. He knew there was something about Monica. She wasn't the average chick. Now he knew what it was. She was supposed to be there. She set him up. It took heart to do what she had done, go through what she had gone through, all for the all-mighty dollar. Oddly, he still wanted her. Even more than before.

"I hate to break this up, but we got to speed this up. Time is not on our side, boo," she said and winked. She then looked at Blue.

"Blue. Blue, oh Blue," she said somberly. "Poor baby," she laughed.

She pulled out the small ceramic container with the battery acid in it.

"Hold him," she instructed Mya.

She forced the chemical down Blue's throat with a long oil funnel. He chocked uncontrollably as the liquid made its way down. Mya could see the acid start to eat through his throat. The smell was foul.

Takela and Kayla walked up and watched as a huge hole formed in his throat. The liquid ate through his skin from inside out.

"You are fucked up," Kayla said at the gruesome sight.

"Okay, we need to go now," Takela said checking her watch.

"Where the fuck is Shay?" Takela asked Monica as they exited the side door opposite from where Calli exited earlier.

The made a clean escape up the street toward the Nissan Maxima they used as the getaway car.

"I don't know. She was right in front of me, then when I looked back up, she was gone," Monica said

"Call and see is she alright," she instructed Kayla.

"Hello?" Shay answered.

"What the fuck happened? Where are you? Are you okay?" Kayla asked, firing off question after question, not giving Shay time to respond.

"Nya. Nya got shot. Sh-She died. I couldn't stay there with her like that. I knew y'all had it from there. That's the only reason I left," Shay said, hurt and full of regret.

Nya finally escaped Blue's clutches, just to team up with them and die the same night.

"What? My sister is dead? She can't be dead. No. Please, no. God why? Why did you let this happen to us? A life filled with hurt, pain, and regret. What type of God are you?" Mya asked hysterically.

Monica rocked her in her arms as she sobbed. The scene brought tears to all their eyes.

"I promised her that once we got out of there, everything would be okay. I promised her that we would live better. That the pain and abuse would be no more. I promised her," Mya cried.

"Shay, where are you now?" Takela asked.

"I'm at home, but it's not safe here, yet. There are police cruisers everywhere. They have the entire street blocked from here to downtown," she answered.

Shay stayed mere minutes from the downtown area. The police setup a perimeter and searched every car that passed.

"Where is Nya?" Mya asked in a voice filled with hurt.

"I had to leave her," Shay said.

"I left her at Emory University Hospital. She was dead when I brought her. I waited until they had her in before I left," Shay said sadly.

Mya didn't respond. She just cried.

"Shay, call us as soon as your street clears," Takela said.

"Okay, be safe you guys. I love y'all," she said then ended the call.

She had just made it to her home minutes before they called.

She went in and checked on Jaz who was still asleep. She gave Jaz some medicine through her IV and let her rest.

She noticed that few items out of place. She kept a photo album in her kitchen drawer, but it was on the counter. She knew she hadn't put it there, but she waved it off, assuming she probably did, but just didn't remember.

Shay had been feeling very sick lately. She couldn't hold any food down and was always nauseous. Her menstrual was like clockwork, at the beginning of every month, but it was now the end of the month and she still hadn't had a cycle.

She had gone out earlier that day and purchased a pregnancy test. She put it up to take it later. She grabbed the test and went to the bathroom to take it. The minutes it took before the results reflected on the screen felt like hours, but the minute they can back, Shay thought she would faint. She held onto the sink with her mouth wide open. Two lines showed on the screen confirming her suspicions.

She heard noise outside of the bathroom door. She then heard a loud bump. She opened the door to the bathroom and was met a 9mm pointed directly at her forehead.

"Calli."

Chapter Thirty

"So, it was you all this time," Calli said. He glared at Shay with pure hate in his eyes. Calli threw the picture of her and her girls in Mexico the year before.

"Y'all set this shit up from the beginning, the whole time. You knew this bitch? Damn," Calli laughed. "We should've seen this shit coming. None of this shit started to happen until you and that bitch came along. Where is all the money y'all stole from the traps?" he asked.

"Calli, I'm so sorry. I never meant for this-"

"Bullshit!" he yelled, making her jump. "Don't fucking stand there and lie to me. Explain her to me," he said pointing toward the room Jaz was in.

"I'm so sorry, Calli. I wasn't going to hurt you. I was going to make sure you weren't harmed. I would never hurt you, Calli," Shay said.

"You just killed my brother, Shay!" he yelled. "How the fuck can you stand there and say some shit like that," Calli said, full of emotion.

He was hurt beyond words. He wanted to shoot her. He wanted to strangle her. He wanted to beat her. He wanted her to take him to her friends so he could do the same to them.

Unbeknownst to the other men, Calli and Blue were half-brothers. They had the same dad, both kept their father's secret.

Calli admired the fact that his father never treated him different. Even though he was married to Blue's mom, he still took care of his son, giving him the best of everything. At first, Calli felt some type of way about him going home to Blue's mom. He felt like he was only getting half of his dad. His feelings changed as he got older when he finally understood his dad.

Calli hated to admit that he had fallen in love with the woman standing before him, especially after finding out who she really was. All this time, he thought he could spot a snake in the grass miles away. But he couldn't spot her. He hauled off and slapped her so hard that she flew back into the bathroom. He followed her and stood over her, still pointing the gun in her face.

"Please, Calli don't do this. Please, I love you. I never meant to fall in love with you, but I did. I couldn't help it. Please, I can tell you feel the same way. Please, I can make this right," Shay begged.

"You can't make this right," he said, deciding to kill her.

"Calli, wait. I'm pregnant. Please, it's yours Calli," she quickly said.

"Bitch, do I look stupid to you?" he yelled.

"I just took the test. It's over on the sink. Look. Please, just look," she cried out.

Calli picked the test up from the counter and read it. He could not believe what he just saw. He was angry and confused. He didn't know what to do at that point. He couldn't know for sure if it was his, but he knew there was a possibility. Killing her would be killing his child. He couldn't bring himself to pull the trigger.

He paced back and forth, deep in thought, as if Shay wasn't there. He wanted to avenge his brother. Since he couldn't kill her, he wanted the other girls involved. Shay watched as a disturbing calm came over him.

"Did Jaz have anything to do with this plot?" he asked.

"No. Monica met her when she was there. She knew nothing of our plan. She has been in there asleep since she left Blue's house," Shay answered.

"Where are the others?" he asked.

"Um."

"Don't fucking play with me. It's either them or you," he said coldly.

"Please Calli, don't do this."

"I'm only going to ask you one more time. Where are the others?"

Shay hesitated. Calli pointed the gun back at her.

"Okay, I'll tell you. Please, don't kill me," she said.

Shay told Calli everything about her girls. She told him where they were from and who hired them to take down their empire. She even told him how much they were paid for the job.

Calli couldn't believe what he was hearing. Shay appeared so innocent. He would've never guessed this was what she did.

Looks can be so deceiving, he thought.

Chapter Thirty-One

"Why has it been so long since we kicked it?" Monica asked.

Since the job in Atlanta, three weeks ago, the women had all seemed a bit too preoccupied with life to hang out. Each woman had meet her quota and was now ready to look for a new career, or hobby, depending on who you asked.

They split everything evenly and included Jaz and Mya. Jaz and Mya had gotten along with the group.

They were all at Takela's house for dinner. Her birthday was a week away, and she wanted to discuss her plans. Normally, she would have planned months in advance, but she had been super busy lately.

She'd really missed her girls. She had great news and couldn't hold back her excitement.

"I don't know, girl. Life has had me occupied," Shay said.

"Me too," Kayla said.

"Well, guess what?" Takela said.

"What?" the women asked in unison.

"I'm going to be a mom," Takela announced excitedly.

They hugged Takela while congratulating her.

"How far along are you?" Kayla asked.

"Three months. I was wondering why I had been feeling so sick. I found out when we were in Atlanta, but I wanted to confirm it with my doctor, before I said anything," she explained.

"I know Mason is ecstatic," Shay said.

"And you know it," Takela said smiling.

Mason had been acting bitter because she lied to him. But, when he found out about the baby, he quickly forgave her. He didn't want to put any stress on her while she was pregnant. He catered to her, hand and foot. She enjoyed every minute of it, too.

"So, are you still considering retiring from this?" Shay asked Takela.

"Yes, ma'am. I have a little one to look out for," she said.

"That's what's up," Shay said.

Takela noticed that Shay seemed angry once she found out that she was pregnant. She also noticed that Shay had been distant all night, but she waved it off. Shay was like that sometimes. One day she would be all bubbly, and the next day she would be anti-social.

Shay had yet to tell anyone she was pregnant. It would raise too my questions that she wasn't ready to answer. She was now two months along. She and Calli were still seeing each other on the low.

He was still hurt by her actions, but he loved her. He couldn't bring himself to cause her any harm. Not while she was carrying his seed, anyway. Having a child on the way gave him a very different outlook on life.

He still wanted revenge for his brother's death, and he would get it sooner rather than later. But he wanted to walk away from it all afterward. He had stacked well over thirty million in a Swiss bank account, so he could afford to walk away.

After what happened in Atlanta, he relocated to Mississippi to be closer to Shay. Only a select few knew he was alive. He didn't want her girls getting wind of him being this close until he was ready to make his move. The element of surprise was always the best way to go.

Shay had been feeding him bits and pieces of information about their whereabouts. He could tell she really didn't want to do it, but she chose love over loyalty.

"So, what are your plans for your birthday? I know you have something extravagant planned," Kayla said.

"Not really. I want to rent out Club Push in the Horseshoe Casino," Takela said.

"Like I said, extravagant," Kayla laughed.

"That would be cool. They have four levels with huge pools on each level. The dance floors are made of glass and they have glass elevators overlooking the dance floors. It's really nice in there," Monica said.

"Yeah, I know. That's why I want to throw my party there," she said.

"Have you spoke with the managers there?" Monica asked.

"Yes. I'm going down there tomorrow to pay," she answered.

"Y'all bitches better be ready to get y'all party on," she said.

**

After the loss of her twin, Mya felt like a part of her was missing. It hurt her deeply to bury her sister. She was all she had left. Sure, the group welcomed her with open arms and had treated her like a sister, but she still felt alone.

Jaz had healed fine. She was too strong to be broken by Blue. She had a strong heart. There were scars on her heart, but none visible to the eye.

She enjoyed being with the girls. She had never had many friends. In school, most of the girls were jealous because she was beautiful, and the boys were just mad because she wouldn't give them the time of day.

Each woman's beauty matched the other. It was hard to say who looked better than who in the group, because they were all drop dead gorgeous. So, there was no room or reason to hate at all. After they came back to Memphis, Kayla agreed to let her stay with her until she was comfortable enough to be on her own.

Takela let Mya stay with her. They knew the two women would need time to heal and adjust, so they were giving them all the time they needed.

"All right, chicas, I'm headed out. Love y'all," Kayla said. Jaz followed.

"Alright, you guys, be safe," Takela said as each woman left.

Chapter Thirty-Two

The next few days were filled with the women preparing for Takela's birthday bash. She went all out for her big day. She planned a red-carpet event with Chanel décor.

"Girl, you should've considered becoming an interior designer. You could've made millions, honey," Monica said.

She had always admired her girl's decorating skills. She could turn a piece of shit house into a lavish mansion. She looked around the club at the many beautiful balloon arches.

"I need you to put that here," Takela said to one of the workers she'd hired.

"Why the hell did you hire them if you're not going to let them do their jobs?" Kayla said laughing.

Takela had been rearranging everything they did. She found something wrong with everything they'd made or touched.

"They could've sent me somebody else, because these here don't know what the fuck they are doing," she hissed walking over to fix one of the balloon arches that was now slanted.

"Well, I'm not done shopping yet, so I have to go," Kayla said.

"Bitch, what you mean you not done shopping? You have to first start shopping with your last-minute ass," Takela said.

"Bye!" Kayla yelled.

"I'll see you guys later tonight," Kayla said leaving.

Jaz, Monica, and Mya helped Takela finish decorating.

***

"What time will Takela get there?" Calli asked Shay.

"We will be arriving together. We'll be on the scene no later than 10:30," she answered.

"Cool," Calli said.

Calli called in a few of his men from Atlanta to help him carry out his mission.

"How are you feeling?" he asked Shay, noticing she was a little pale.

"Not good. This baby has me in shambles. I can't keep anything down. I tried saltine crackers and ginger ale, but even that comes up," she said.

"Poor baby," he joked. "You'll be okay," he said kissing her lips.

"Yeah, you would say that. You don't have to go through this miserable process," she said.

"I go through worse. A pregnant woman will have a man growing grey hair. I got a few strands already," he said laughing.

"Shut up," she said and hit him with the pillow.

At first, she felt bad about feeding her girls to the wolves. But as each day passed, her guilt slowly faded. She loved her man and was willing to do anything to keep him. Her girls couldn't fuck her, or

166

keep her warm at night. That was, unless she wanted to go gay, but the chances of that were slim to none. There was nothing in this world that could take the place of dick, or the man that's slanging it. Dildos would do nothing for her.

She was supposed to be meeting the ladies at Takela's house to get ready. They would all leave from there. Mason chose to leave earlier to ensure that everything was perfect for his wifey.

The women were lounging around as night slowly approached. They were reminiscing about old times.

"Shay used to be the one we had to make fight," Monica said.

"That girl would let people talk to her any kind of way and wave the shit off. I hate that shit," Takela said.

"Good thing we broke her from that," Monica said.

"Remember when Bre kept picking with her in the cafeteria? She would pick with her because she knew Shay wasn't a fighter. She had the nerve to bump her, making her drop all her shit. I told Shay's ass she wasn't leaving that damn cafeteria until she handled that bitch," Takela explained.

"Aw yeah, I remember that," Monica said laughing.

"When Shay saw that I wasn't playing, she took off her backpack and got in Bre's face. Next thing, I know Shay knocked the shit out of Bre. That bitch hit the ground instantly," Takela said.

"Then Shay just struck out," Monica said.

"Huh?" Jaz said.

"She ran. Everybody was dying laughing. I was like what the fuck is she running for? Shit, where the hell is she running to? She had gained some cool points until she pulled that shit. Bre's ass was still on the ground," Takela said holding her stomach laughing.

"I give it to her, though. After that day, she didn't take no shit. Ha retarded ass would beat a bitch if she waved," Monica said.

"Speaking of Shay, where the hell is she? She was supposed to be here hours ago," Kayla said.

"You know how she get. When she say she is on her way, add an extra two hours to her arrival time," Takela said.

She looked at the clock and saw it was a little after nine. Time had flown by.

"Damn, it's 9:07 already?" Kayla said.

"Come on. Time to slay," Takela said just as Shay walked through the door.

"Y'all ain't ready yet?" Shay asked as if she was ready her damn self.

"Bye Felicia!"

Chapter Thirty-Three

**Club Push was popping. Everyone who was anyone was in the building. The night was young, but there was already a line wrapped around the building.

There was a long red carpet in front of the club, roped off. Only VIP guests were allowed to walk the red carpet. At the entrance, was a huge red and black balloon arch. The banner in front of the club read, "Happy Birthday, Queen Takela."

Takela and her girls pulled up in a black on black Mercedes-Benz S-600 Pullman. They killed the scene as they stepped out and walked down the red carpet.

Takela wore a short McQ Alexander McQueen red bondage midi dress with red and black stilettos. Kayla wore a Michael Kors red lace one shoulder cut-out asymmetrical bodycon dress with matching red stilettos. Monica wore a red Dolce & Gabbana halter backless front cut-out strappy bodycon dress with matching pumps. Jaz wore a La Petite Robe di Chiara Boni red and black multi wear panty embroidered dress with black pumps. Mya wore a red Jimmy Choo lace club dress with matching Jimmy Choo pumps. Shay wore a red Vestidos Pu Leather Hollow lace backless dress with black pumps.

They killed it, and they knew it. They could see the envy and hate in the chicks' eyes as they walked past. They ate it up too. They posed for a few pictures and made their way in for Takela's grand entrance. There were four bouncers at the door.

Inside, there were red and black balloon arches strategically placed around the club. There were photo booths setup with the Chanel theme in the background. Each table had Chanel red tablecloths and Chanel center pieces. The elevators where decorated in the red and black Chanel theme as well. The pools were filled with red foam with red and black balloons placed in and around them.

She had personal bars setup in each VIP section, so everyone in VIP had their drinks brought to them. All drinks were free in the VIP area. There was a seafood buffet setup a few feet from the bar.

"Alright, stop what the fuck y'all doing and let's welcome one of the baddest chicks in the building!! The birthday girl!! Queen Takela!!!" the DJ announced.

The club roared in applause as Takela made her way to her throne with her name above it. Mason meet Takela at the door.

"Happy birthday, baby," he said and gave her a long, passionate kiss.

"Get a damn room," Monica said and smiled.

"We already got one upstairs," Mason said and winked.

They headed toward their section and took their seats. Takela wanted to scope out the scene before she hit the dance floor. She couldn't believe the turnout. She wondered if they were over the capacity. The bartender came up and took their orders for drinks.

"Let me get a Sex on the Beach," Shay said. She knew she shouldn't be drinking, but she was going to need one to make it through the night.

"I'll have what she's having," Jaz and Mya said.

"I'll have a virgin daiquiri," Takela said.

"Let me get a martini," Monica said.

"Me too," Kayla said.

The bartender nodded and left to fill their orders.

They nodded their heads and looked at the down at the dance floor. The DJ was playing Future and Drake's *Used to This*.

After they had gotten a couple of drinks in their system, they were ready to hit the dance floor. When the DJ played Rihanna's *Work*, Takela pulled Mason to the dance floor. They grinded on each other as if they were fucking on the dance floor. The DJ switched it up and played Rihanna's *Love on the Brain*. Takela wrapped her arms around Mason's neck and began to rock and sing along.

At that moment, standing in his arms, she knew that was where she always wanted to be. Mason kneeled on one knee in the middle of the dance floor and took Takela's hand in his. The DJ stopped the music, and a guy walked up and handed Mason the mic.

"Takela, my queen, I have loved you since the day I met you. I'll never stop loving. You are the woman I want to spend the rest of my life with. I promise I will do everything I can to keep a smile on your face. I promise I will never intentionally harm or hurt you. Most relationships fail due to lack of communication, so I promise to always keep a line of communication open with you. You have stood by me through thick and thin. Will you marry me, my Queen Takela?" Mason asked.

"Oh my God, Mason baby, yes. It will be an honor," she said.

He slid the five-karat round, three-stone engagement ring on her finger. Everyone applauded as they exited the dance floor.

"Real man type of shit," the DJ said and turned the music back up. Mason held her in his arms as they looked out at the crowd.

POW! POW! POW!

Takela and Mason both hit the floor. **

The crowd erupted in chaos. People were stumbling over each other to get out of the club.

Kayla and Monica ran toward Takela after they noticed she had fallen. Jaz and Mya followed suit.

"Oh my God, Takela!" Monica panicked.

Takela lifted up, in shock. She turned around to see Mason laying on the floor bleeding.

"Mason!" she yelled. "Mason baby, get up!" she yelled.

He slowly lifted his head.

"Baby, where are you hit?" she asked.

Mason looked down to see he was hit in his shoulder and side. He had on a bullet-proof vest so the shot in his side only stung a little.

"I'm okay, baby," he assured her.

POW!

Mason's brain matter flew all over Takela.

"Ahhhhhh, Mason!' she cried out. "No baby, you can't leave me. You promised, baby. Ahhhhh," she continued to scream.

The women looked around frantically, trying to locate the shooter. Monica spotted Shay on the other side of the club with the smoking gun still in her hand.

She was shocked beyond words.

"S-Shay," Monica stuttered.

The women followed Monica's gaze and looked directly into Shay's eyes.

"Why Shay? Why?" Takela cried.

She couldn't be heard over the crowd, but she read her lips.

Takela then saw a man walk over to Shay and instantly recognized him as one of Blue's boys. The women stood still for a few moments, trying to register exactly what was going on. Then rage took over.

"Bitch!" Takela yelled as she took off down the stairs toward Shay. Before she made it halfway down the stairs, she saw the four bodyguards from earlier surround her.

"Fuck," Kayla said realizing they left their guns in the car.

They had no weapons on them because they weren't expecting any problems. They'd left everything in the limo.

Takela ran toward the first man, continuously swinging on him, but he blocked her punches. The other guards just stood around laughing.

Then Takela discreetly pulled her blade from its thigh holster and swung. The man grabbed her hand before it could connect, a mistake on his part. The blade went through his hand. He yelled out in agony.

Takela used that as an opportunity to snatch the blade out and stuck it in his throat, killing him instantly.

Mya grabbed one of the wine bottles from a nearby table and smashed it against one of the bouncers' heads. This only seemed to infuriate him. He ran toward her and Mya grabbed a piece of the glass and began to stick him in his chest until he was no longer moving. She looked animalistic covered in his blood.

Monica and Kayla ran up on the third guy. Using the bottles around them as weapons. They repeated what Mya had done.

Jaz grabbed one of Takela's blade and sent it flying toward the fourth guard's eye. He screamed when the knife connected. She ran up, snatched the knife, and cut his throat.

When Takela looked back at Shay, she saw her and Calli going toward the exit. They grabbed the men's guns and ran after them. When they made it to the parking lot, Shay jumped in her car sped off.

Takela snatched the keys of a young woman who was clearly getting the hell out of dodge threw the guns in and followed Shay

❖

"You did good baby," Calli complimented.

Shay smiled and sped up. She thought she was losing them until she saw Takela come around an eighteen-wheeler truck.

"Shit," she said.

"Nah, bitch, you not getting away that easy," said Takela driving like the mad woman she was.

Shay crossed over three lanes all the way to the Perkins exit and took it.

"Haha bitch, better luck next time," Shay said.

"Fuck, she exited," Takela said.

She couldn't get over, so she had to drive down to the Getwell exit. The street was empty at that time of night. She couldn't tell where Shay had eased off to. She drove around for an hour looking for her. She knew that Shay was smart enough not to go to her home, so she didn't go that route. She cruised down Perkins slowly looking for the car.

"There it is," Mya pointed.

Shay's car was sitting in the parking lot of a shopping plaza.

"Why the fuck would she be in there?" Takela asked.

'Beats me," Jaz said.

"Maybe this is where they stashed a getaway car," Mya said.

175

The entire plaza was empty and Takela knew Mya was right. The pain from the events of that night was unbearable. She was trying to wrap her head around why Shay would cross them like she had. She didn't understand. She kept asking God why he allowed her to take her heart and stomp on it. She drove away from the plaza with a heavy heart.

I guess when it comes to dick, loyalty plays second fiddle, she thought.

Chapter Thirty-Four

Takela hopped back on the expressway headed home. She knew they couldn't go back to the club because police would be swarming it.

"Over there," Jaz said as she spotted Shay's car. Takela stayed back, not wanting to risk Shay spotting her.

She followed Shay until she reached the Germantown exit. She watched as Shay pulled into the Marriot Hotel.

"I can't believe this bitch," Kayla said.

"What the fuck is he doing to that bitch, 'cause ain't no dick nearly that damn good that it'll make me betray y'all, my sisters. What the fuck is wrong with her?" Monica said as they watched Calli kiss Shay and walk hand in hand toward the entrance.

"Yo, Calli," a man called a few cars down from Takela's car.

The women ducked. They were close enough to hear the entire conversation.

"Did you find them?" Calli asked.

"Nah, but when we got to Kayla's crib ha man was there, but that nigga fucked up now. He put up a hell of a fight, though," the man laughed. "Them bitches bound to come home eventually, and when they do, my guys will be there waiting," he said.

"Cool. I need every last one of them hoes bodied," Calli ordered. "Tonight!"

"I got you, brah. You still trust her?" the man whispered to Calli.

"Fucking right. She has proven where her loyalty lies," Calli said. "Find them," he said and walked back to the hotel entrance.

They picked up their room key and went to their room.

"They're in room 413," Mya said.

"How do you know?" Kayla asked.

"I read the receptionist's lips. But if you're questioning it, just call the front desk before they make it to their room. That's the only way you'll get their room number," Mya said

"Thank you for calling the Marriot. This is Amanda," the receptionist said.

"Hi, Amanda can you connect me to LaShay Walker's room," Kayla said.

"Um, she just came in. I'm not sure if she made it back to her room or not. One moment," she said.

"Okay, she hasn't made it up yet. She's in room 413. So, when you call back just change the last four digits to 0413, and it'll connect you right to her room. Is there anything else I can help you with?" she asked.

"No, that'll be all. Thank you. Bye," Kayla said.

"Mya, you and Jaz stay here and keep lookout. This bitch gunning for us, so more than likely they may have someone watching.

178

Them niggas will stick out like a sore thumb. If anything pop off, you know what to do," Takela said.

Both women nodded.

Monica, Takela, and Kayla grabbed their guns, entered the hotel and took the elevator to the fourth floor. The receptionist was too busy fumbling with her phone to notice the blood covered women enter. They got to the fourth floor undetected.

"I'll be out here if you need me, boss," they heard a man say as the elevator doors opened.

When the man turned and looked into Takela's eyes, he was met with a bullet to his right eye.

Three other men hit the corner. Takela noticed them from outside in the parking lot talking to Calli. They started to fire toward her rapidly. The loud gunshots began to wake the other patrons of the hotel. They started to scream from inside their rooms, but were too afraid to come out, for obvious reasons.

Shay's hotel room door opened and Takela could see the chrome tip of a SR Ruger stick out. Calli fired toward Kayla. One of the shots pierced Kayla's side and the other pierced her shoulder. He aimed for Monica next, but his gun jammed.

Takela used this as an opportunity to force her way into the room. She delivered a fierce kick to his dick and he dropped. She kicked him again in his face. She snatched his gun and ran past him toward the bathroom.

Monica fired two shots into Calli's knees, dropping him where he stood. She sent another bullet through his hand.

"Bitch!" Calli screamed.

Monica swung the gun at his temple.

"My." *Whack!* "Name." *Whack!* "Is." *Whack!* "Monica," she said as she delivered another blow with her gun to his temple. He was no longer moving.

"Hurry up and get here," Monica heard Shay scream into the phone.

"I'll be back for you," Monica said, and walked to the bathroom.

Chapter Thirty-Five

As soon as Takela spotted Shay, she dropped her gun and ran toward her. She wanted to beat the shit out of her before she killed her. She punched Shay in her nose and then the throat.

When Shay bent over and held her throat, Takela kicked her in the face.

Shay was quick on her toes as she caught Takela with a punch to her eye and then kicked her in her stomach, causing Takela to double over in pain. She then kicked Takela in the face twice.

"Get up, bitch," Shay said.

When Takela tried to stand back up, Shay kicked her in her stomach.

"Get up!" Shay said again.

Again, Shay kicked her in the stomach and laughed.

Takela was trying to catch her breath and ignore the ache in her stomach. She knew if she wasn't on the verge of having a miscarriage, she would be if she didn't get off the floor.

She spotted a liquor bottle on the floor a few feet away from her. She balled up and began to scoot away from Shay.

"Tough ass Takela giving up so quickly. Wow," she laughed.

"Bitch, ain't nowhere to run. After I stomp that bastard out of you, I'm going to put two bullets in your head. Bitch, you think you can have your happy ending? No, bitch. Poor, poor Mason. Loved the wrong bitch," she teased.

As Takela positioned herself directly in front of the bottle Shay asked, "You know what I think of you? Huh?" then she spit in Takela's face.

Takela gripped the bottle tightly in her hand and swung with all her strength smashing the bottle against Shay's temple, dazing her. Shay stumbled back, allowing Takela the time she needed to regain her composure and stand. She grabbed a huge piece of glass from the broken bottle as she stood and charged toward Shay.

She swung, cutting Shay's face from under her eye down to her lower jaw. Shay screamed in pain and tried to grab the glass, but Takela was too quick. She swung again, but Shay threw her arm up trying to block her face, causing Takela to cut a long gash down her arm.

Takela dropped the glass and pounced on Shay. She delivered vicious blow after blow to Shay's entire body. Shay could fight, but she knew she was no match for Takela. Takela went from punching her to stomping her.

"Takela, you need to hurry up and finish this bitch. We don't have much time," Monica said from the doorway.

"Lookout!" Kayla screamed, snatching Monica out the way just as a gunman let off two rounds. Monica instantly fired, hitting the gunman in the center of his head. Two more men rounded the corner and were each met with a bullet to the dome.

"You okay?" Monica asked Kayla

"Yeah, but this shit hurts like hell," Kayla said holding her side.

"Where the fuck is Jaz and Mya?" Takela asked.

Just then, her phone rang.

"Takela, we are surrounded," Mya yelled.

Takela could hear gunshots in the background.

"The more we drop, the more come," Mya said as she eased up on one of the gunmen and shoved a blade in his throat. She snatched his gun and looked back to see Jaz right behind her watching her back.

"They are coming in the building heavy. They shot the receptionist and are headed your way now," Mya said.

"They're already here," Takela said as she took out another one of the men and took his gun.

"We need to find a clear escape route," Monica said. In her peripheral, she saw Shay running up behind Takela.

"Takela!" Monica yelled.

Takela looked back in time to see Shay coming toward her with a blade. She noticed a gunman aiming for her, too. She fired toward him and ducked, then fired at Shay as she leaped behind the nightstand for cover.

She hit Shay in the stomach. Shay dropped to the ground face first. Just as Takela aimed toward Shay's head, her gunned jammed.

"Fuck!" she screamed.

"Takela, come on," she heard Monica say.

Monica gave Takela another of the two guns she had taken from the men. Kayla picked up a gun located by one of the gunmen's head.

"Y'all ready?" Monica asked as they prepared to finally exit the room.

"Yeah," they answered as they made sure they had a bullet in the chamber.

Monica kicked the room door open, and they exited the room. They were met with over a dozen masked men with guns aimed at them.

They all fired simultaneously. Takela aimed for everything moving to her right while Monica shot everything moving to her left, and Kayla aimed for everything in front of them.

They made their way to the stairs without being hit.

"Fucking amateurs," Monica laughed.

As they were walking down the final flight of steps leading toward the side exit, the door was kicked in and they were met by more gunmen. They both aimed and fired, only to hear their guns click.

The men laughed.

"Looks like y'all will be leaving with us," one of the men said.

"Pull the car around," he said into the phone.

Pow! Pow! Pow! Pow!

Takela watched the head of the man on the phone split open and his men followed.

"What the fuck are y'all just standing there for?" Jaz yelled.

The sirens in the distance made them put some pep in their steps. They hurriedly got into the car and sped off.

Chapter Thirty-Six

Six Months Later

"Oh my God, she is so adorable," Monica swooned over her new niece.

Takela gave birth to a beautiful eight pound, twelve ounce baby girl whom she named Miracle. She was her father's spitting image.

She had only been home fifteen minutes before her house was packed with loved ones bearing gifts and congratulations.

Although she missed Mason more and more with each day, looking at her daughter made her heart smile at what she and Mason had created. She knew he was smiling down at her.

After the whole ordeal with Shay, Takela went into a deep state of depression. It was Monica's idea for them to take a trip overseas to get away from it all. They were only supposed to be gone for two weeks, but two weeks turned into a month and a month turned into four months.

The women only rushed back after the fourth month so Takela could deliver in the States. She knew that after she reached her thirty-sixth week of pregnancy, she would not be permitted to fly.

After the trip, she was slowly able to pick of the pieces of her life. She took it day by day. After she delivered her baby girl, she had a reason to smile again. She chose to be strong for her baby girl, because she knew that's what Mason would want.

"I know," she smiled and kissed her baby.

"Let me see my niece," Mya said.

"Look now, don't spoil her. Don't hold her when she's sleep," Jaz said.

The girls laughed.

"Alright, Mother Tares," Jaz joked.

After a while, the crowd cleared out and Takela and her girls started to straighten up a bit. They helped Takela finish her daughter's room.

"Alright, chica I'm gonna call it a night. If you need anything, just call," Kayla said.

She hugged her girls and left. The rest of the crew kicked it with Takela for the remainder of the night until they fell asleep in her living room.

Takela jumped up from her sleep when she heard what sounded like a door opening. She went to check on her daughter to find her sleeping peacefully. She waved the noise off, assuming she was just paranoid.

She went into her bedroom and stretched out on her bed. Before long she dozed off. She was jarred awake again a few minutes later when she heard her daughter began to cry. When she made it to her daughter's room and went to pick her up from her crib, instead of seeing her daughter in her crib, there was only was a baby monitor there. She could hear her daughter crying on the monitor. She then noticed the window was open.

"Ahhhhhhh, my baby!" she screamed, waking her girls who ran to Takela's aid to see why she was screaming.

"Someone took her," she cried. She picked up the monitor and ran toward the front door with her girls right behind her.

She could still hear her baby crying and knew she wasn't far. As she made it to her front yard, she saw a Honda Civic parked in front of her house.

"This is my baby, now," Shay said into the baby monitor.

Takela could see Shay smiling sadistically in the front seat, holding her baby. Calli was in the driver's seat.

"Goodbye, bitch," Shay said and then Takela's house exploded and Shay sped off. The explosion threw the women across the yard and into the street.

It took the women a few minutes to recover from having the wind knocked out of them. Had they not followed Takela out the door, they would all be dead, instead of suffering minor lacerations from the blast.

"Noooooooooo!" Takela yelled, watching the Honda turn off her street. She ran toward Monica's car, but each car exploded before she could make it, sending her flying back once again.

To Be Continued….

Please be kind and leave a review▯

CPSIA information can be obtained
at www.ICGtesting.com
Printed in the USA
LVHW051657011020
667693LV00010B/986

9 781545 536933